THE
JEWEL BOX

A Capitola Mystery

by

Mysty W. Moonfree

Published by Women of Mystery—A Capitola consortium of readers, writers, painters, mah jonggers, knitters, and various other rapscallions of literature, art and culture.

Dedication:

The Jewel Box is dedicated to women
Who enjoy reading mysteries
And dream of someday writing one.
It is possible, even if you need four friends
To write it with you!

Acknowledgments

WHEN FIVE WOMEN OF A "CERTAIN" AGE agree to give birth to an entirely new creation, for them—a book—support comes from many corners of their worlds.

Women writers traditionally acknowledge their long-suffering husbands, saying they couldn't have done it without them. Well, we'd like to make it clear that we did do it on our own, and we deeply appreciate their behind-the-scenes encouragement.

Kathryn Gualtieri was a wealth of inspiration and help. Special thanks not only for her writing skills, but also for helping to create the story line and to develop the characters.

Four additional Women of Mystery attended our earliest meetings in 2003. Their input helped consolidate our thoughts. Thanks to Mary Vaage, Peg Ogg, Tracy Armanino and Molly Ording.

Once we five finished writing and our intensive editing, we each asked someone to give our book a critical read. For this valuable help, we thank Kathryn Gualtieri, Carolyn Swift, Julie Lambert, Bob Newman and Susan Goldstein.

Sophia Varcados created a beautiful map for us. Judith Feinman took the amazing cover photo and Lisa Hindley added her expertise to the cover design. Carolyn Swift, the director of Capitola's Historical Museum helped with historic descriptions, reading and photography.

Joe Ortiz emerged as our hero. As did other husbands, Joe read and critiqued The Jewel Box, then to our amazement he graciously took over the huge task of preparing the book for its first printing.

And we thank our book group, the Capitola Women of Mystery for bearing with us over the past four years and, basically, leaving us to our task. They are: Jennifer Chase, Margy Cottle, Marsha Gonzales, Carin Hanna, Vinnie Hansen, Helen Slater, Ann Stagnaro, Marion Stoops and, in memory, Sue Porter. They were curious when at one point we confessed we still did not have an ending; they were supportive when we huddled in discussion, while others were sipping tea, munching dessert and waiting for our monthly club meeting to start.

Introduction

Mysty W. Moonfree is an anagram for Women of Mystery, the name of our book club, which has been meeting since 1993.

Five years ago, after reading a particularly unsatisfying book, we all decided it would be fun to try writing something ourselves. We wondered if we could rise to the challenge of collectively writing something that would be suspenseful and just a darn good read.

Immediately, we knew the book had to be set in Capitola, where many of us live.

It has been an involving process that took us in many directions before we settled on the book you will read.

We began with thirteen members willing to give it a try. Then, eight members bowed out, either because of time constraints or realizing that group writing wasn't for them. So we became a team of five writers. That's when the real work began. There were countless meetings, figuring out the next step in the story, who would write what chapter, how a character would develop. Over time our voices came together, as well as our spirits.

What delights us all now is the camaraderie and joy that came out of this process. It's been a true melding of the minds of five women who wanted to see how this story would end. Week after week, month after month we plowed on, enjoying every step of the way. And best of all, we deepened our friendships.

Marybeth Varcados
Pat Pease
Judith Feinman
Tomi Newman
Gayle Ortiz

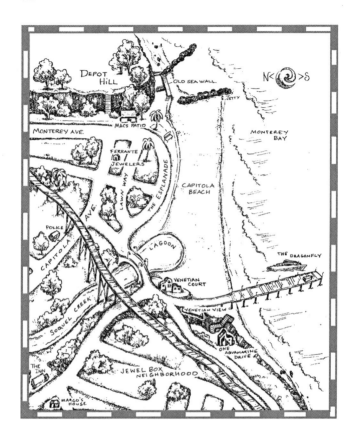

CAPITOLA VILLAGE

THE
JEWEL BOX

A Capitola Mystery

Prologue

Even in late August, Monterey Bay was never warm. The afternoon sunlight had raised the water temperature to a mere 63 degrees, so Adrian and Roxanne took just a quick swim around the gleaming hull of the Dragonfly. The previous night they had motored along the California coast, dropping anchor at daybreak at Capitola-by-the-Sea.

Shivering, Adrian grasped the metal ladder at the side of the vessel, pulled himself onto the deck and reached over the rail for Roxanne's hand. He guided her toned body up and tossed her a beach towel.

Adrian's talents for designing exquisite jewelry attracted well-heeled women. As he slipped into a terry cloth robe, he turned to admire Roxanne's firm, youthful figure. Somewhere in her early fifties, she was naturally beautiful, and wore no makeup. Her body was tanned and slender under her see-through lime green shift. Her only obviously unnatural feature was the long, platinum blonde hair that she'd drawn back into a ponytail after their swim.

Adrian signaled his chef to serve lunch. For the next hour, the couple relaxed on the secluded rear deck, enjoying freshly caught halibut, watercress and goat cheese salad, with a Napa Valley Chardonnay from the ship's wine cellar.

Roxanne folded her napkin and leaned forward. She toyed with the star-shaped diamond pendant dangling from a platinum chain encircling her neck. "Adrian, darling, who is this Dana person you've picked to join our group tonight?" she asked. "I hear she's politically connected."

Standing behind her, he bent and planted a kiss on the back of her neck.

"You're my shining star, darling. I'll never make another jewel like yours."

Designing and creating Roxanne's uniquely shaped pendant had been extremely difficult, he remembered. He'd presented the dazzling jewel to her during his holiday house party eight months ago. She was the envy of every woman in the room that night.

She scowled. "You still haven't told me about Dana. Why? I've had the strongest feeling since Christmas, Adrian. I know this diamond has powers of illumination, and right now, it's telling me I'm about to be replaced."

He grabbed her ponytail and jerked her head back playfully. "Enough, Roxy. You hear me? Enough."

"Stop! You're hurting me." She pulled away from him and quickly excused herself to go below.

A thick fog settled over the Dragonfly's deck. Adrian was distracted briefly by the boisterous sounds of loud music and noisy laughter coming from the bar scene along the Capitola Esplanade.

IN THE SKY OVER MONTEREY BAY, on a flight path bound for the San Jose airport, Karin Blake pushed her coach seat into its full, upright position. Within the hour, she'd be in Capitola-by-the-Sea, to hand deliver the Jewel Box to Adrian Ferrante.

One

In the week since her fiancé's murder, Karin Blake had lost her appetite. Hunger came and went at odd hours and she'd yet to reestablish a routine. Spending a few days with her twin sister Jennie in Pasadena had been a good idea. Being on the LAPD's list of suspects didn't help, even though she had a tight alibi.

Mark was stabbed in the bedroom of their shared cottage while she'd been moving through a crowd of Hollywood glitterati wielding a tray of luscious hors d'oeuvres. He had been scheduled to work that night, too, but called in sick. Karin didn't know he wasn't coming until she arrived at the sprawling Bel Air mansion. He'd spent most of the day at various auditions and must have returned home sometime after Karin left at 5 p.m.

That night had more to do with this plane flight than Karin could possibly imagine.

She remembered so well the moment they met at a friend's party in West Hollywood. Last place I expected to meet a straight guy, she thought, but there he was, right next to her at the sushi bar. Drop-dead gorgeous. He was in black that night—and so was she. Leather jackets, in fact.

"What's your favorite?" he asked. "Mine's the ahi." My favorite too, she recalled. One delectable bite of sushi led to another, and pretty soon they were toasting with warm sake. He was looking for work. She suggested Golden Catering; they had an opening. He offered, "Want a ride home?" She'd come with a friend, but answered, "Love it." She wasn't sure who started it, but soon they were kissing and one sensuous move led to another and pretty soon they were on her bed. He brought her coffee in the morning. They sat in the sun, reading the Times and observing life along the Venice Canal. Not long after, he moved in. And was hired on at Golden's.

They agreed to keep their relationship secret. Two short years ago.

Karin straightened her spine and took a deep breath. Oxygen. Maybe that would help her relax.

LEANING OVER THE EMPTY SEAT to Karin's right, the flight attendant asked in a low voice. "Would you care for something to drink?"

The flight to San Jose would be less than an hour. Few passengers traveled mid-day, and most had their laptops open, catching up on dot-com work. Karin shifted her attention from the port side window.

"Orange juice, thanks."

WHEN THE ATTENDANT HAD GONE, Karin pulled her carry-on from under the seat in front of her and retrieved a plastic bag containing apple slices. Though she didn't much feel like it, she'd better eat. She had a lot to do today.

She turned back to the window. The Mediterranean landscape was a perfect backdrop for replaying that morning's meeting with Georgia Golden, LA's reigning Queen of Caterers, in Georgia's tasteful office above Wilshire Boulevard. Georgia had been her usual bitchy self.

"You're a good worker, Karin, but I'm not running a modeling agency or a charity. I can't have someone who looks anorexic representing Golden Catering. Put some weight on."

"I've got plenty of energy, Ms. Golden, and I need the money."

"That's not the point."

"It is for me," Karin shot back. "Look, I could work in the kitchen."

Georgia glanced toward the door, anger flickering in her large green eyes. Karin turned and saw Georgia's handsome husband, Enrique. "Heading over to the kitchen," he called out. "Can I bring you anything, hon?"

"No," she snapped.

Enrique smiled despite his wife's hostile reply and closed the door as soundlessly as he'd opened it.

Georgia moved from behind the large antique desk, reforming her face into something resembling compassion.

"I know this is a tough time for you."

"You have no idea," Karin replied.

Georgia continued as if she hadn't heard. "We all miss Mark. You're young, Karin. You'll bounce back."

"So, I'm being fired. Is that it?"

"I never said that," Georgia forced a smile.

"I have another job for you," she said. "There's a party at Adrian Ferrante's in Capitola tonight. I want you to deliver his Thank You Box and make sure everything is set up right. You don't even have to work the party."

It wasn't the best offer, but she needed the work and it seemed easy enough. Mark had done these deliveries, she recalled. Not that long ago.

One little touch that set Golden Catering apart from the rest of the upscale caterers in town was the small, jeweled box of exquisite chocolates hand-delivered to each client the afternoon of their party. The bonbons were made of the best Belgian chocolate, pungent liqueurs and imported French butter.

Karin grabbed her handbag and went downstairs to the kitchen to retrieve the box. It was particularly beautiful. The top featured a nosegay of violets made of amethysts surrounded by jade leaves, all nestled on hand-dyed lavender shibori silk.

She was now a delivery person, she thought bitterly, and she didn't even like flying.

When the flight attendant brought her juice, Karin lowered the tray in front of the empty seat, nodding thanks, and turned her thoughts back to that morning.

After her unsettling conversation with Georgia Golden, Karin put the top down on her '78 red Karmann Ghia and took her time getting home to her Venice Beach cottage. Plenty of time to reflect on her life which, at 32, was going nowhere fast. A degree in journalism from San Jose State and a two-year stint in a couple of small Southern California newspapers had proved to her she wasn't cut out for an occupation that fed on the sensational side of people's lives.

Disillusioned, she decided to work for Golden Catering just long enough to catch her breath and decide on a new career. That, to her parents' dismay, was three years ago. The only good thing to come of it was meeting Mark. Now it felt like her life would never get started. On the car seat next to her was the box of chocolates, Georgia's answer to keeping her behind the scenes.

She hated going home. Images of Mark's murder were jagged shards in her memory. She unlocked the door, entered the foyer and went straight to the kitchen. She'd better keep the little box cool. Karin made herself a Virgin Mary and went to the bedroom to start packing. High on a closet shelf was Mark's suitcase. She decided to use it, to feel closer to him.

Grief and loneliness washed over Karin.

She longed for the touch of Mark's strong fingers on the back of her neck rubbing out knots of tension after a long night of catering. She missed his slanted grin reflected in the mirror as he watched her put on her morning makeup, or his demand for a kiss before she applied her lipstick. She missed his enthusiasm for barefoot strolls along the Venice Beach shoreline at sunset. How had she survived the unreality of the last week? It was a blur. She sighed deeply, blinked back tears, and reached for his suitcase.

She noticed the light blinking on the message machine. "Hi Mark, this is Wolf Camera. You'd better pick up your photos. They've been here for a few weeks now."

Mark must have sent them in before he was murdered, she thought. Photography had been his passion; he insisted on using high-quality film instead of digital. When he wasn't trying to get an acting audition or working parties for the Goldens, he was shooting pictures.

ON HER WAY OUT OF TOWN, Karin stopped by Wolf's and picked up two photo packages, along with an extra card for her digital camera. She turned the Ghia onto the 405 Freeway and headed toward LAX.

Her cell phone rang; Enrique Golden's voice crooned, "Hey Babe! Como estás? Just wanted to see if everything's okay. You looked upset in the office. Are you okay?"

"I just picked up Mark's last photos from the camera shop. That's a downer, and on top of that, Georgia took me off serving and reassigned me to shit work."

"She tell you why?" he asked.

"I look anorexic. Not good for the image of Golden Catering."

A cross between a laugh and a grunt rumbled in his throat.

"God, she's a hypocrite. Most of Georgia's clients are either famous or criminals. Remember last week's party for Congressman Burleigh?"

"Sure. The mansion in Malibu. Great view."

"Well, the wife complained about you. Said she didn't want murder suspects serving her guests. Of course, if O.J. was in town, he'd have been at the party schmoozing with Burleigh, his old golfing buddy. Thing is, until Mark's killer is behind bars, Karin, you're a liability."

"A liability with bills. Georgia's not the only caterer."

"Sorry, kiddo, not in this town. At least not for a while. The word's out—spread by Georgia. She doesn't want you to get comfortable with another caterer. You're the best server she's ever had. You don't distract the guests."

"Oh, not too pretty, you mean," Karin interrupted. But, she reassured herself, not being one of the tanned, toned and toothy set populating LA didn't concern her. She wasn't going to be around here long.

"You're efficient, babe, and you don't use the job to buttonhole producers to sell your screenplay or get a part. Just do what she asks and hang in there."

THE FLIGHT ATTENDANT CAME BY for the last time, asked her to raise her seatback and helpfully returned the tray to its locked position.

As the aircraft made its final descent to San Jose, Karin began to feel uneasy. Perhaps it stemmed from her brief conversation with the detective leading the investigation into Mark's murder. Per instruction, she'd called to tell Detective Ishiguro she'd be spending the weekend in Capitola. He absently thanked her, and when she asked if there were any new leads, he abruptly asked how long Mark and Enrique Golden had been friends. She replied truthfully that she never knew them to be friendly at all. The detective thanked her again and they rang off.

The Fasten Seatbelt sign flashed, and she suddenly remembered the photographs. She had just enough time to look at them before the plane landed.

Reaching under the seat, she pulled them from her carry-on. The first couple of pictures were of her, not great shots but she knew she would save them. It was the last day she and Mark had spent together. He'd caught her laughing, just as a wave broke over her Boogie board. After several similar shots, she saw the face of a woman she didn't know. She was stunned.

Karin estimated the woman to be about 25, blonde and slim. She was over-the-top glamorous, wearing a pale ecru dress cut low and sexy. So attractive, Karin thought, polished and classy. Obviously, she spent a lot of time on her looks.

She wore a large, stunning necklace, a thick gold chain holding a spectacular jewel. Karin wasn't sure what kind of stone it was, but figured it was wildly expensive. The woman was on a beach unfamiliar to Karin. She was smiling coyly, her mane of hair thrown over one bare shoulder.

The next few photos were variations of the first. Karin's skin prickled and her heart sank. What the hell was going on? She'd thought her relationship with Mark was strong, but maybe not. She put the remaining photos back in their package, too heartsick to look further.

As the plane taxied toward the terminal, Karin decided she'd best compartmentalize her growing sense of unease.

She needed absolute focus on the job at hand, which, in any case, looked simple enough.

She checked her watch and calculated: by 3 o'clock, she'd be in Capitola, having delivered the Thank You Box to the client and checked into her hotel. She'd be free later to ponder the significance of the detective's question and, more important, to think about the photos.

TWELVE YEARS HAD COME AND GONE since Karin last visited Capitola, but her memories were vivid. As her rental car sped over the Highway 17 coastal range, details of those salty summers with her family put a smile on her face. She was anxious to see if California's first seaside resort had changed.

Entering the village, she was happy to see that the benevolent hand of progress had not squeezed Capitola too tightly. The Skee Ball Arcade was gone, so was the merry-go-round, but the cozy small town feel was still there.

Ferrante's Jewels was near the beach in the ocean-side village. Nestled in a palm-lined avenue famous for its unique shops and galleries, it was hands-down the best-known jewelry store on Monterey Bay.

Three generations of Ferrantes, all named Adrian, had maintained the family tradition of excellence. Known for one-of-a-kind, rather large but classic creations their pieces had an unmistakable cachet. The current Ferrante, a grandson of the original Adrian, was handsome, charismatic and, above all, famous for his luxurious parties.

Karin parked the rental car and deposited two quarters in the meter. It was good to be back in Capitola. The aroma was unmistakable, a combination of the sea and French fries. She'd spent many happy summers here, waterlogged and sandy.

Approaching the shop, she refocused her attention. Her hand grasped the doorknob. As she glanced through the top of the polished walnut Dutch door, she froze. Inside the shop the two clerks were chatting. One was an older, well-dressed woman. The other, to Karin's complete astonishment, was the young blonde in Mark's photographs.

Two

THE JEWELRY CASES WERE CHOCK FULL of sumptuous pieces, all well out of Karin's price range.

Pretending to be interested while trying to figure out how she would handle the situation, she kept her head down. Obviously, Mark had met this woman while in Capitola working one of Adrian's parties. As she was imagining several scenarios, the older sales clerk interrupted. "I see you've found the new line of sapphire necklaces. Quite stunning, wouldn't you say?"

The woman didn't recognize her; Karin had never worked at Adrian Ferrante's parties. "Well, yes," she answered, "but I'm here on business, unfortunately."

She held out the jeweled box, which the sales clerk recognized immediately.

"Oh you must be Karin from Golden Catering. I'm Margo Shepherd. Ms. Golden phoned to say you would be delivering the Thank You box and setting up. Just put it over behind the counter. I'll deliver it to Mr. Ferrante's home."

"I'm afraid I can't do that," Karin replied. "You know, Enrique always likes them delivered in person. One of the company's personal touches. 'Hand delivered' he always says."

Karin glanced into the mirrors lining the wall behind the cases just in time to see the blonde approaching. The girl looked sheepish and averted her eyes. Up close she was even more stunning than in the photographs. Her youthful complexion was flawless. Movie magazines would describe her as having "bedroom eyes." Trying to contain her growing anxiety, Karin extended her hand.

"Hi, I'm Karin Blake," she chirped with what she hoped was a convincing smile.

"I'm Summer Shepherd, Margo's daughter," she answered nervously.

The mother stepped in. "You must be tired from the flight. Would you like directions to Mr. Ferrante's house?" Not waiting for a reply, she retreated to the back of the store, saying something about jotting down the directions for Karin.

Trying not to appear flustered, Karin blurted matter-of-factly, "So, I understand you knew Mark Hansen."

"Not really. I asked him to take some professional photos of me. We had lunch on the beach, that's all." Her face reddened. She seemed nervous.

Karin wondered. Did the woman know who she was and her relationship to Mark, or was she jumpy because of the murder?

"I hardly knew him," Summer continued. "Really! Saw him a couple of times when he was here doing parties."

The marked physical difference between them was not lost on Karin. She'd never been considered a beauty and, standing next to Summer, she felt like the proverbial ugly duckling. Her short stature and spiky, black hair didn't add to her confidence.

"Well, it was good to meet you," she said. "I'll be heading for Mr. Ferrante's now." She took the directions from Margo and left the shop as fast as she could. Back in the car, she felt light-headed and slightly sick to her stomach.

Her grief over Mark now was combined with pangs of jealousy she wasn't even sure the situation warranted. How could her life go from a smoothly running, if not idyllic, existence to this? Okay, she told herself, just keep pushing forward, no time to think about this now. She scanned the directions and proceeded over the bridge, up a steep hill overlooking the creek that ran to the ocean just behind her. Once up the hill, she turned left and found herself in a familiar neighborhood.

The Jewel Box was one of Capitola's prime locations. Perched above the municipal wharf jutting out into the bay, homes on the cliff had sweeping views considered by many to be the best in the area. Of course, One Aquamarine Drive, the Ferrante home, was the largest. It sat behind an ornate iron gate, the gabled roof of the coral-colored Victorian just visible above a cluster of eucalyptus trees.

Karin rang the bell at the gate and watched as a remote camera focused on her. "May I help you?" It was a woman, probably one of the housekeepers.

"I'm Karin Blake with Golden Caterers to deliver the Thank You box and help set up."

The buzz startled her, but she quickly pushed the gate and stepped inside. The landscape around the house was given over to the natural flora of the California coast; ferns and various shade-loving perennials proliferated in the meticulously manicured surroundings. Beyond, the bay hung brilliant, like a perfect plein air painting.

She walked around to the servants' entry, as instructed. As she entered, she heard the shout of "Four bam, two crak" coming from the cook, who sat with other household help, embroiled in what looked like a game of Mah Jongg. They barely noticed her entry. The cook pointed to the large commercial refrigerator in the butler's pantry. "Just put it in there."

Karin ignored the instructions and slipped into the next room, looking for Mr. Ferrante. Once inside these beautiful homes, Karin couldn't resist peeking. The dining room was particularly opulent. Tapestries, possibly Italian Renaissance, covered every wall that didn't have a window with sweeping views of the bay. The round, Chinese lacquered table was almost twelve feet across, with ten chairs beautifully upholstered in cinnabar Asian brocade. A collection of specimen orchids and another of ivory Netsuke completed the overall impression of old money.

A carved ebony secretary in the corner groaned with a collection of old photos. Karin's eye caught a familiar face in one of them. There was a young Georgia Golden amid a group of stylishly dressed people, smiling broadly, in an opulent ballroom. Her arm was linked with that of a handsome man. The caption read, "QE I update—Young Los Angeles caterer-to-the-stars feted on the occasion of her 25th birthday by family friend, Capitola jeweler Adrian Ferrante." They looked quite cozy, thought Karin.

Just as she was ready to continue her search, Karin heard a man's voice in the next room. Although the door was closed, she could tell it was a phone conversation, and not too friendly.

"This has been a long and very satisfactory relationship, wouldn't you agree? Let's not get greedy and foul things up, shall we?" The man's tone became patronizing. "These endeavors take time and an abundance of patience. If you try to rush things, neither of us will realize the full potential a project like this can offer."

Before she had a chance to move out of the way, the door opened and hit her on the back. Adrian Ferrante stood at the threshold with a look that made Karin want to disappear. He was tall, at least six feet, trim but definitely not slight. What a hunk, Karin thought, and cosmopolitan. No doubt, a world traveler. He wore black linen pants cut close to the body. His cerulean blue silk shirt was obviously hand-made; it fit like a glove.

Karin looked up. His eyes were clear blue, with a piercing quality. His tan skin was well maintained for so much time out in the sun. He combed his black hair straight back, sleek and shining. The scent of his cologne flooded the room. Karin found it indescribable.

She noticed the huge multi-toned ring on his little finger. What were the stones, she wondered.

This was a man who knew his place in life and flaunted it. He was simply mesmerizing. What a package, she thought.

He continued his phone conversation as if she weren't there. "Just calm down and follow my lead. Remember, this was my idea in the first place. I can find another source that will be more than happy to do things my way. Do I make myself clear?"

He hung up without waiting for an answer.

"Who the hell are you?" He finally acknowledged her.

"I'm so sorry, Mr. Ferrante, I'm Karin Blake from Golden Catering. I was coming to deliver your Thank You Box."

"Just leave it on the table. In the future, kindly announce yourself when you enter this house. I don't like people sneaking around," he bellowed.

"Yes sir, I'm terribly sorry," Karin said quietly.

She slipped into the foyer and out the front door. That kind of behavior never surprised her. She'd seen it dozens of times while serving parties in elegant homes. People with his kind of money and connections often were demanding and rude. But this guy was at the top of the class.

Even so, it was hard to dislike a man who made your knees weak when you looked at him.

ADRIAN FERRANTE MADE SURE she was gone, then moved to the table. Opening the box, he took one of the chocolates and popped it in his mouth. It was his favorite, filled with Grand Marnier. The boxes were always fantastically decorated. He had to admit, they were one of the reasons he loved the caterers. He placed the box on the table and removed the rest of the chocolates. His fingers found the familiar tab of fabric on the inside edge. He pulled up the floor of the box. A smile began to appear, showing his perfectly whitened teeth. Now *this* was what he'd been waiting for.

Three

DRIVING BACK DOWN THE HILL, Karin noticed a small cottage with a fringe of tall, bright blue hydrangeas. The old-fashioned flowers, tucked beside the Victorians, were one of her fondest memories of Capitola-by-the-Sea. Those were the best times with her parents and her sister Jennie. Most days at the beach, Karin wore an inner tube around her waist and floated in the lagoon for hours. Nights were usually spent in the small movie theater, a post-World War II Quonset hut. The theater's frozen Snickers and fresh popcorn were legendary.

She decided to check into her hotel room and catch a nap before setting up the party. The Venetian

View Hotel was just above Capitola's wooden fishing wharf, which dated from the nineteenth century. From her second floor room, Karin had an unobstructed view of Monterey Bay.

She pushed the sliding glass door open and walked out on the balcony. Small pleasure boats were moored at buoys on the water.

Her ears picked up strange marine animal sounds coming from under the pier. She inhaled, appreciating the iodine-rich aroma she associated with living at the ocean's edge.

Leaving the door open, she moved back inside and began unpacking. Tired as she was, she wanted to do one thing before she could even think of resting.

She crossed the room and settled into a wing chair in the corner. Turning on the floor lamp, she reached into her carry-on bag and pulled out the worn piece of newsprint she had been carrying for the past week. Tears welled as she stared down at the headline.

It was the lead story in the LA Times printed the morning of August 18.

Reading aloud those familiar sanitized sentences, Karin's loss and terrible grief overwhelmed her once again.

Actor Murdered In Savage Attack

VENICE, AUG. 17—The body of promising actor, Mark Hansen, was discovered shortly after 11 last night in a Venice Canal bungalow.

Police Detective Dan Ishiguro said that Hansen's girlfriend, Karin Blake found the body on returning home from an evening catering job in Bel Air.

Hansen, age 36, was bludgeoned and repeatedly stabbed in the neck and chest. The couple's ransacked bedroom showed signs of a prolonged struggle.

It was unclear whether the actor knew his attacker. Blake reported to the police that the front door was unlocked when she arrived home.

Contents of two suitcases belonging to Hansen had been disturbed and several items of monetary value had been scattered on the bed and floor. Robbery is not a likely motive for the murder, according to Ishiguro.

The victim was born Marco Hernandez in the town of Encinitas near the Mexican border. He appeared in numerous television commercials and in supporting roles in movies such as "Joyride" and "Never Talk to Strangers."

Ms. Blake could not be reached for comment.

HOW MANY TIMES had she read those words and relived the awful pain of discovering her dead lover? What happened that night would remain with her forever.

Karin had heard the music of a Latin salsa beat when she entered their darkened cottage. But no cheery "Hi, Doll," greeted her. Instead, she found Mark's mutilated body, sprawled on top of a bloodied white satin sheet. Things were in complete disarray. A lamp was shattered. The contents of drawers and clothes closets were scattered about. Even the bathroom shelves were swept clean. Had she seen anything out of the ordinary? Could she remember beyond the horror of it all?

Then it hit her. There was something odd about that night. Mark's favorite Nikon SLR was on a pillow next to his battered head. The back of the camera was open. There was no film in it. When the police searched the cottage, they found no film in his camera bag or with his photo equipment, or anywhere, for that matter.

Where had it all gone? Did Mark's hobby have something to do with his death?

Exhaustion set in. Karin decided to leave the photos for later. She'd had enough for now. She pulled up the blankets and listened to the sounds of the sea lions in the dark waters below the wooden boards of the old wharf. Their sympathetic low moans seemed to comfort her. She slept.

The ringing of the phone awakened her.

"Hi. Karin? It's Summer Shepherd. Can we meet? I know, you don't even know me. But you seem cool and, like, I think you'd hear me. For sure, I can't tell any of the gossips around here. I really need someone to talk to. Please?"

"Sure," Karin could feel the sincerity in the girl's voice. She had a strange urge to be kind to her. "What about after I've set up for the party. Where do you want to meet?"

"You know the bench at the end of Aquamarine Drive, overlooking the wharf?"

"Yes, I've seen it. It's just down the street from the Ferrante home, right?"

"Yeah, that's the one. How about 7:45? Will you be done by then? And, hey, bring something warm. It gets cold out there on the cliff."

"Yeah, I'll be there. See you later."

What could she possibly want to talk about, Karin wondered.

As she dressed for the evening, Karin considered taking another look at the photos, but decided she didn't have time. Leaving the hotel, she put aside thoughts of a big cheeseburger and a glass of zinfandel. She'd sit down to a good meal after her talk with Summer.

She decided to take the five-minute walk up the hill to the Ferrante home. It would give her a chance to clear her head and begin setting the stage for the party. She needed to focus on work now. Babysitting the caterers and servers was going to be a new experience. Maybe this wasn't all bad; maybe she could move up in the company as a manager some day.

Whatever the evening held, she hoped it wouldn't mean running into Adrian Ferrante. She wasn't looking forward to seeing him again.

Four

FLAKY CHEESE PASTRIES were ready for the oven. The Alaskan wild salmon gave delicately to the touch. All was ready for the party.

Karin completed last-minute details and handed the evening over to the Goldens' staff and Adrian's crew, just arriving in their starched white and black uniforms.

"Good work!"

An aspiring caterer from the community college food program complimented Karin.

"Thanks," she murmured, glad she wouldn't have to meet the gritchy Mr. Ferrante again. She grabbed her bag and wrap, and set off to meet Summer.

Much to Karin's surprise and delight, the old weed-studded wood and dirt staircase still descended to the beach. Typical of Capitola's mix of old and new, she mused, as she left Adrian's groomed estate and strolled the timeworn cliff-side path edging Aquamarine Drive. Silently she thanked those who renovated turn of the century Victorian homes, rather than tearing them down and building what someone called "monster" homes.

Lights were coming on in the historic village below. She reached into her bag, pulled out her digital camera and took several shots of sailboats dancing at anchor near the wharf.

The setting sun glinted off the water; the sky was darkening to Prussian blue.

Karin put her camera away and spotted her cell phone. I'd better call Jennie, she thought. I didn't tell her that I would be up here overnight. She would've loved being here too, revisiting our favorite hangouts. Jennie . . . she's so nurturing. No wonder she became an RN. Only twenty minutes older than me, but, boy, can she be bossy. Karin speed dialed Jennie's cell.

"Hi. It's Jennie. Leave a message."

Disappointed, Karin left a brief message to let her twin know she was fine, working for the Goldens in good ole Capitola, and would be home in the morning.

A GLANCE ACROSS THE VILLAGE to the Depot Hill bluffs jolted her thoughts to darker topics. She flashed on a story in the LA Times, probably a year earlier, describing an alleged murder committed off the cliffs. Apparently, the case was still open. Beauty may be skin deep, she thought, but sinister things can lurk beneath. She turned away, heading for the bench to join Summer.

Summer perched on the bench, her silky hair teased by the soft bay breeze. Waves crashed against the cliffs below. The evening fog drifted north across Monterey Bay from the Carmel headlands and cooled the air.

Still in her short, floral patterned skirt and sheer pink top from work, the young woman gave a shiver, and shrugged into her denim jacket. She smiled tentatively as Karin approached, moving her bag to make room for the caterer to sit. Karin, still in work pants, sensible black, and a crisp, white shirt, ran her fingers upward through the ebony spikes of her Annie Lennox haircut. Her wine-dark lipstick had faded to an end-of-the-day smudge.

The younger woman blurted, "So, when I saw you, I really wanted to talk. You know, about Mark and me."

Karin, nonplussed, nodded.

"I know that you guys were living together. And worked together at the deli—I mean catering company—and everything . . . I mean, he talked about you. And the big thing is, I saw that story in the newspaper that day, when mom and me were down at the bakery for morning coffee. And how you found him. I know that. And, well, when you walked into the shop today, I knew it was you."

Summer picked up her tempo, "They think you murdered him but I don't believe a word of it! Do you care if I call you Karin?"

"That's fine. And thanks for not pegging me as a murderer," Karin nearly snarled at the sun goddess next to her, rhinestone-edged toenails and all.

Summer persisted. "Mark came into the jewelry store when I was working. I can't believe it. Wow, it seems like a long time ago. He was bringing stuff from the catering place for Adrian. I told him how I want to be a model and all. Mark was bragging and all about how he's good at photography and maybe would do some PR shots for me. Really. That was it.

He did those pictures as a favor. Nothing else. I have a boyfriend. Of course, he's in LA right now, getting in the movies. But I'm going there, too. As soon as I get the money together, I'll be set. I wasn't going for Mark."

Karin stiffened. "Fine. I don't want to talk about Mark. He's gone. It's over."

She felt her spirits sinking, low, too low to curb tears. She bent forward, head in her hands.

Summer reached out and touched her shoulder. "I'm so stupid, I didn't want to bring you down. I'm sorry."

"Thanks." Karin pulled out a tissue. "I didn't expect to lose it in front of someone I just met. What am I supposed to do? They think I killed Mark. I need help, not girl talk, Summer."

"Well, I'm not all that lame," Summer struggled. "Plus, I think I know some serious stuff. Can I tell you? This sucks. Really. And I need someone to talk to about this. I'm feeling Mark was a part of it."

Focused on the girl, Karin reached into her black nylon bag.

She pushed her camera to one side and pulled out Mark's photos.

"Explain this."

She held out the glossy photo of a stunning young woman wearing the even more stunning piece of jewelry.

Summer saw herself, come-hither eyes, shiny blonde veil, cleavage and, oh, that necklace. "That necklace! That's the one. When he saw me wearing it, he totally freaked."

"What?" Karin was puzzled. "Freaked?" Her suspicions about the two—was she off base? She tipped the photograph, looked critically at the necklace and felt herself drawn to the amazing jewel, fiery with pinks and gold.

"Okay, you won't believe this … I borrowed it from the safe in the jewelry shop." Summer's voice was low. "No one was supposed to know about it. I couldn't believe his reaction, like fear, or something. He said there was more to it, but he wouldn't explain. What was that about? I didn't do anything wrong."

Karin's reporter instincts kicked in. "And? Is there more?"

"It's not just me," Summer confessed, agitated. "My mom said stuff, too, about those sapphires, and how she never saw invoices for some of the goods that came through the shop."

Karin pushed. "Like, what kind of stuff?"

"Mark said not to talk about it. And now he's dead!"

The fog had reached Capitola's cliffs, enfolding them. Protection was what Karin craved; she reached into her bag, pulled out her old red shawl and cocooned herself.

Summer leaned toward Karin and lowered her voice.

"I hear those women bragging about their jewels. They come from all over the place to party at Adrian's. And they're just all gaga about Adrian and what a fox he is. They're so pathetic, all drooling all over him and everything."

STARTLING THE TWO WOMEN, a kid on an obnoxiously loud pocket bike sped toward them, and Summer shouted, "Beat it, Surf Rat."

"Up yours, lady." came back at her. "Where am I supposed to ride? We're not allowed on the streets." Leaving dust, he took off, and for the first time all day, Karin's face softened and she smiled.

A little.

DIGESTING WHAT SUMMER had told her, Karin shrugged. "I don't know anything about the jewelry business.

Maybe that untraced stuff is part of another business, maybe under another name."

She was feeling her way. "The Ferrantes are old Capitola. The daily newspaper keeps track of local businesses. I bet there's a file on them a mile thick, both business and social. I could probably dig through those files, or the librarian will help me. You never know."

"Look," she continued, "I'm going back to LA tomorrow, but if I can get my name off that suspect list, I could get back up here and do a file check on the Ferrantes. I'd love to play detective for a day. How about it?"

Karin would return to Capitola sooner than she suspected, but there wouldn't be time for a trip to the local archives.

"HEY," EXCLAIMED SUMMER. "I just flashed on this. Let's go see my mom right now. She's cool. And she's tight with Adrian. And her house is really close. Maybe she'll have a clue."

It was nearly dark as they headed toward Emerald Street and Margo Shepherd's.

Still hesitant to trust her own emotions, let alone trust this gorgeous girl walking briskly beside her,

Karin pondered. What was I thinking, hooking up with this kid? Stop it, woman. Just be cool; keep your ears open. I hope this doesn't hurt me. God, I wish Mark was here right now. Anyway, at least it feels like I'm doing something—anything—not just sitting on my ass. Who knows, it might help. Would be great if it shed some light on Mark's murder.

At the corner of Aquamarine and Emerald, a woman rushed by, pulled by a small dog on a leash. The short, spiky-haired caterer and the tall blonde turned in unison, curious.

The woman barely glanced at them, as if they were invisible.

Karin stiffened, leaned to Summer and softly, as if to herself, murmured, "That's Dana Burleigh, the LA congressman's wife. What's she doing up here?"

Summer watched as the woman turned toward Adrian's house.

"Adrian's women are staying at the new Inn on Soquel Creek. Maybe she walked over; it's just on Wharf Road. She's probably going to that stupid party."

Five

THE MARINE LAYER HOVERED along the coast. Dana Burleigh and her tiny Yorkie, Buddy, walked through the gate and admired the pond edged with abalone shells. The sound of a mellow jazz piano drifted into the evening, the melody confirming the guests' suspicions that each one of them was "Lovely—just the way she looked tonight."

It was an unusually attractive group of women who were assembling on Aquamarine Drive for Dana's induction into Adrian's very exclusive society. Dana handed her Pashmina wrap to the maid who greeted her and walked into the already crowded entry. From the corner, the Michael Feinstein sound-alike at the piano looked her over, winked, then blushed as he realized he'd seen this face in the political pages of the paper, and she was not just another of Adrian's Suchin Society cuties. Adrian left Roxanne's side and immediately enveloped Dana in a warm hug.

"Dana, darling. I'm so glad you're here. Come meet some of my dearest friends. I know you'll like them because they share your generous heart as well as your love of my finest jewelry. I'm thrilled to bring you all together to support my charity. I love designing a special piece of jewelry for each of my beautiful girls. You'll adore the ruby piece I've done for you— it's fabulous!"

Behind her social smile, Dana wasn't overawed. He's really laying it on thick, she thought, scratching Buddy's ears.

He led Dana to an animated group of women and began introductions. Every woman wore a distinctive, opulent piece of jewelry, each bearing the unmistakable look and artistry associated with Adrian Ferrante's internationally known designs.

The designs were various, drawn from natural elements—shells, flowers, birds and animals—and all made liberal use of precious stones hidden in the curves and swirls of gold. Adrian always managed to include the initial of the wearer. Thus, brunette Elodia from Miami wore a brooch in the shape of a leaping dolphin heavily encrusted with aquamarines with her initial "e" cleverly forming the dolphin's eye. Loretta, whose husband controlled an agricultural empire on the central coast, wore a pin with overlapping emeralds forming the leaves of an artichoke, with a lower-case "l" tucked between two leaves.

Tonight Dana would receive her first piece of jewelry, crafted from rubies. She was curious and excited to see what Adrian had envisioned for her. Her indulgence was a secret kept from her fond but frugal husband, who viewed her love of adornment as far too elitist for his political goals. When Adrian invited her to be part of his "Society," Dana told John about the worthy charity she would be involved with, but she had deliberately omitted any mention of jewelry.

ADRIAN, HAVING SEEN TO THE COMFORT of his chatting guests, picked up a glass of champagne and walked out to the edge of his property. From the cliff he could easily see the wharf and his true love: The Dragonfly.

He'd purchased the boat from a Southern California broker. A classic eighty-foot yacht built in 1964, it was outfitted for scuba diving and deep sea fishing. The cachet for Adrian was that it once was owned by a

Hollywood mogul, who entertained movie stars aboard. With his fine eye for design, Adrian had it refitted to his specifications, down to the smallest detail.

He sipped the champagne, remembering his last year at Stanford. Damn, I was an ace in architecture. Would have made it, no problem, in grad school. Teachers loved me. And the impeccable social connections at Stanford. Then Pop gets sick and Mom, always the controller, demands I come back and help at the shop. I thought, okay, just for a while, then I'd get out and make my mark in the world.

He sighed heavily. Man, I'd love to get away from all this. Sell the family home and business. Get on the Dragonfly and escape to Cabo. Maybe cross the Pacific to Hawaii, maybe Tahiti.

"Ah, well," he said to no one in particular. "Let's get on with this party. See how our new guest is doing. And I'd better check on Roxy."

STANDING BY A HIGHLY LACQUERED Chinese table, Roxanne eyed the iced bowl of caviar. Using the little mother of pearl spoon, she ladled a generous portion of the tiny eggs onto a toast triangle and popped it in her mouth. Bursts of briny flavor brought a smile to her lips.

I love Adrian's parties, she thought—good food, elegant champagne and wines, music, fun-loving company, and Adrian himself. Like many genuinely attractive men, he had the gift of focusing on you so intently that it felt like you and he were alone in the room—alone in the universe, perhaps.

Then she remembered how he had yanked her hair aboard the Dragonfly. So hard it hurt. She frowned. He's beginning to lose his charm, she decided. She fingered a petite chocolate creampuff. To hell with calories, I need this.

Idly, Roxanne picked up the handsome brochure outlining Adrian's Suchin Society. Sad-eyed Thai orphans pleaded for help from her affluent American self, peering out from the thick, matte pages. An architect's rendering of a light, airy building promised a happy home for the children, thanks to her generous contributions. On one page, a photo of Adrian, virile in an open-necked shirt and impeccably tailored slacks. On the facing page, photos of some of his most alluring jeweled pieces.

Then came text that appealed strongly to his carefully evaluated customers. Entry into his exclusive group would cost $10,000. In return, the inductee would be given a unique ruby piece as a thank you.

Each year the donation was to increase, and a jeweled creation with correspondingly increased value would be received. For the second donation of $25,000, the stone was a fire opal; for $40,000, emeralds were to be used; $75,000 would merit diamonds; and the ultimate, final donation of $100,000 would result in the gift of an unusual, mysterious stone whose powers, it was hinted, would give the wearer renewed vitality and youthfulness.

Ha! Cynically, she drained her glass.

Turning back to the drawing of the proposed orphanage, Roxanne mentally calculated how much money had been donated by this group, with no photographs of a completed building yet to be seen. When she had suggested to Adrian that the two of them fly to Thailand to see the site and meet some of the children, he stroked her cheek and suggested they spend some time together cruising on the Dragonfly.

"I know how lonely you've been since your husband died, Roxy," he'd whispered, pulling her close. Touched by his tenderness and excited by feeling his body pressed tight against hers, she happily changed the subject.

The cruise up the coast left her physically satisfied, but oddly, she now seemed to be spoiling for a fight.

Maybe it was seeing Adrian being so attentive to the dark and lovely newcomer, Dana Burleigh. Dana was a lot more sophisticated than most of the other women. In spite of good looks and wealth, they were not a worldly group, thought Roxanne. There was a lot of new wealth, which often left these women on the fringes of more established, old money society. Here, they felt special and truly appreciated.

Adrian certainly was appreciating Dana. Roxanne grabbed another flute of Veuve Cliquot and headed for the bathroom to check her makeup.

"Are you all right?" came a voice from behind Roxanne. In the mirror she saw Dana Burleigh, looking even better—and younger—up close.

"I saw you bolt into the bathroom and I thought perhaps you were ill."

Oh great, the woman was a Florence Nightingale, too. "I'm fine," snapped Roxy.

Startled by Roxy's venom, Dana took a conciliatory approach.

"Isn't it wonderful, this project that Adrian dreamed up? For an artist to take on a cause like this is remarkable, I think. And he's so enthusiastic, he can hardly wait to get started."

"Started?" Roxy moved back near the doorway, annoyed by this newcomer's eagerness. "Started? By now, with all our contributions, there should be three orphanages, maybe four."

She took another sip of champagne and leaned toward Dana. "You know, Mrs. Congressman Burleigh, I'm beginning to think there may be no orphanages at all—zero, zip, nada. Dear ol' Adrian may be scamming us and all we have to show for it are the jewels. Maybe our so-called donations are making him richer than Bill Gates! What do you think?"

Suddenly she felt a hand clamp her shoulder, like a vise.

"Ooh, baby," hissed Adrian through a charming smile. "I think you need a little fresh air. Excuse us, Dana, and please go try the smoked salmon. I caught the salmon myself."

With that, he steered Roxanne away from the bathroom and out the door toward the pergola at the cliff's edge.

"Roxy, love, I'm losing patience with you. This is Dana's first time here. It's her big night. Why spoil things with your crazy ideas?"

"Are they so crazy?" asked Roxanne. " Nothing's been built yet, has it? And I'm about ready to fork over $100K of my late husband's hard earned money for those precious little big-eyed orphans we never get to meet. And this stone—this Rispinite. Does it really exist, or is it all bullshit?"

Adrian's eyes glittered and his tone was hard. "Roxanne, it's obvious you've had way too much to drink. Why don't you sit here in the pergola for a while and take a few deep breaths. Maybe the ocean air will bring you back to reality. Meanwhile, I have guests who need me. Now close your eyes and I'll give your neck a relaxing little massage."

Roxanne swayed and closed her eyes. In the dizzying darkness she felt his strong, warm hands close on her neck.

INSIDE THE VICTORIAN, the party was gaining momentum. A few women leaning on the piano, drinks in hand, sang along with the romantic ballads. Dana eyed a squirming Buddy with some anxiety and headed for Adrian, who had just come in from the side garden.

"Buddy needs an airing, Adrian. Do I have time to take him out before dinner?"

"Absolutely," he checked his watch. "It's 9 o'clock. Dinner is about 15 minutes away. Just pick up after him, please—Capitolans are militant about doggy doo."

"I'll come with you. I could use some fresh air," put in Charlotte, a statuesque brunette from Atlanta.

Dana admired Charlotte's brooch, a golden sheaf of wheat sprinkled with topazes, her initial "C" forming the knot in the cord binding the bundle. Together the women headed into the increasingly foggy night, Buddy on his leash trotting beside them.

"Let's take the steps down to the beach," Dana suggested, and led the way down the old wooden steps. Once on the sand, she released Buddy and watched him scamper off. Breathing in the tangy ocean air, she summoned her best party small talk and made conversation with Charlotte. Suddenly both paused as they heard a loud, frantic barking further down the beach.

"Buddy!" shouted Dana. She took off running, shoes in hand, toward her dog. She could see the Yorkie yapping next to a shapeless form beneath the cliff. She stopped, looked again. It was a woman, a woman sunbathing when there was no sun. Her neck bent at an unnatural angle, her long hair fanned out on the sand.

Speechless, Dana stared down at Roxanne.

Six

MARGO SHEPHERD LIVED in a typical 1930s Spanish revival bungalow. Karin remembered the style from long-ago vacations, and her mother's years as a real estate agent. She could visualize the inside floor plan before entering. A two-bedroom one-bath cottage with the front door leading directly into the small living room and a tiny eat-in kitchen just beyond.

A tidy, artistically landscaped front yard greeted them. Roses, hydrangeas and several varieties of lavender edged the path to the bright, Chinese Red front door. Wind chimes smoothed the ch'i for their arrival.

Margo was surprised to see them together. "Look what sailed up to my house, the Owl and the Pussycat! Hi, hon. Hello Karin. Come on in. I'll brew tea, or how about a glass of this fruity little wine I picked up at Trader Joe's 'Honey Moon.' Ha! This is as close as I'll ever get to one, at this rate."

Summer laughed. "Tea, Mom. I'd love a cup of that organic green tea with jasmine. And don't give up, there's plenty of men out there."

To her surprise, Karin's stomach began to growl. She hadn't eaten in ages. Hungers, physical and emotional, washed through her. She needed comforting.

As if on cue, Margo said softly. "Are you all right, dear? You must be starving, or does your stomach always growl at strangers."

Karin relaxed, smiled at this gracious woman in turquoise. Mandarin lounging pajamas, how very Capitola. Perfect silver strands through her ash-blonde hair.

"Come into the kitchen. I just made my special Eggplant Parmesan Casserole. I'll heat some for both of you." Karin thawed. "Yes. Thanks. I'd love something to eat, and tea would be fine."

Margo moved gracefully around her kitchen. Herb garlands dried from a low rafter. Primary colors of vintage Fiesta ware lined the open cabinets. Her stove, Karin noted, was an early Wedgwood, complete with a woodburner for foggy Capitola mornings. The woman understood good living. She settled next to Summer at the table. "Has your Mom always lived in Capitola?"

"No," Summer responded. "She had me when she lived in Mendocino. Then, after she and dad divorced, she went through EST training, and began a new life. She heard Capitola was a great beach town for raising kids. So here I've been since I was six. Mom started working for Adrian's father right after we moved here. When I was 10 or so, Grandpa Ferrante made her bookkeeper. I loved Papa Ferrante. He wasn't anything like his pathetic son."

Summer's gaze wandered from her mother to a small jade ring on her right index finger. "Papa Ferrante made me this ring. He was great at jewelry design. He let me start working part time when I was a junior. The job's okay, but where I really want to be is modeling jewelry, not selling it," she sighed wistfully. "I can just see it: Summer the Super Model! Anyway, it's a chance to learn about stones and all."

She turned to Margo.

"Mom, here's why we came over. I told Karin about the store and the jewelry, and how Mark got mad at me, and all. And about those stones that're not entered into the accounts."

Margo served two dishes, one cobalt, the other amber, with a generous serving of the casserole and a few baby greens. She set them before Karin and Summer.

"Mangia. Mangia." she encouraged, then paused.

"Well," she began. "Working for the Ferrantes has been my life for fourteen years. Sometimes, I feel I'm part of the family, you know, included at Christmas, great bonuses. Their great health plan.

"Adrian and I were together a lot for years, him so wild, me trying to make it on my own. Two survivors. Summer, remember when he took us out on the Dragonfly? We had so much fun together.

"Then about two years ago, Adrian began to change, grew a little distant from me. I thought it was my fault sometimes, that I was growing too old, and he obviously had many younger women as friends. After all, I am only an employee."

She paused, then added, "Honey, nothing to worry about. The store's doing just fine, and anything between me and Adrian is past history. Enjoy your dinner, girls.

"I can handle whatever comes along."

Karin thought about Summer's anxiety. "Could he possibly have another business, under another name?" she asked.

Margo quickly denied that suggestion. "No. Not Adrian. He's third generation in the store. I trust the Ferrantes completely. Anyway, I would have picked up on something like another business. But it's true about the cost of the pink sapphires and other stuff not being entered in the books. I can't imagine the cash flow, where the jewels are coming from, where the money is going."

Summer fiddled with her hair, in and out of a pastel scrunchie. "Mom. Like, how long has this been going on?"

Margo sighed. "Honey, don't worry about it. Everything is fine."

Karin hardly touched the food in front of her. This was intriguing. She took a deep breath. "I don't envy you two, knowing all this. If I didn't have so much on my plate," she looked at her dinner, now growing cold, "I could get interested. Unfortunately, what I need is to clear myself in Mark's murder."

"Look," Summer grew impatient. "That necklace. In the picture. We know it had a very rare pink sapphire. That's why Mark freaked out."

Karin pushed her plate away. "I just can't believe this. He never told me a thing."

The three sat quietly. Karin leaned back, closed her eyes and tried to think clearly. Summer obviously was upset. A bit scared? And Margo ... she sensed that Margo was holding back, probably about her relationship with Adrian. Possibly more.

Seven

YELLOW TAPE MARKED OFF the area of the beach around Roxanne's body. The medical examiner was already at work. Adrian, who had called 911 after Charlotte's breathless announcement, stood with his arm protectively around Dana's shoulders.

Dana cuddled Buddy and shivered uncontrollably, partly from the shock of finding Roxanne's body, but also fear of publicity that was sure to follow the tragedy. John would be furious to have her connected with anything so sensational and negative.

She huddled closer to Adrian and whispered. "Can't Buddy and I go up to the house now? I'm so cold."

"Let me talk to Mickey," Adrian replied. Giving her shoulder a reassuring squeeze, he approached the police chief, standing a few yards away.

Mickey Brooks, five feet six and slightly built, was Capitola's first female chief of police. She felt that responsibility keenly. No one who came within range of her acerbic wit questioned her intelligence, or doubted who was in charge. She had made it a point, upon arriving in Capitola, to meet the movers and shakers, from council members to the business owners, whose shops lined the village streets. She was on a first-name basis with many, including Adrian. As he approached her, Mickey greeted him with a question.

"Ms. Reynolds was a guest of yours, Adrian? I'll need to talk to you, and you know we'll need to speak to all your other guests. I've sent an officer to the house to let them know they'll have to stay put."

Adrian acknowledged this with a curt nod. "The lady who found Roxanne would like to go on up to the house and get out of the cold. She's pretty shaken up."

"That's okay," Mickey replied. "We've got a statement from her and we can finish with her up there. Just warn her not to go anywhere. I need to hear what you know. What happened here? Mrs. Burleigh said that Ms. Reynolds was angry when she left the house, and that you and she had words. That so?"

"Women are easily upset," Adrian replied, then remembered that Mickey, too, was a woman, although he had never seen her lose her cool. "Also, she'd had quite a bit to drink," he added hastily. "I didn't want her to spoil the party with her childish behavior, so I walked her out to the pergola to get some air. We talked a bit and she seemed to calm down. I thought maybe the sea air would sober her up, so I told her to stay there for a while. I went back to the party. Next thing I knew, Charlotte came tearing up to the house, screaming about a body. God, I can't believe this. She was . . . she was a shining star."

Mickey eyed Adrian. "Why was she so agitated?"

Adrian snorted.

"It was a woman thing," he said, and then thought, oh God, I've done it again.

"Well, what I mean is, Roxanne and I had come up the coast on my boat together. I think she was feeling a little possessive about our relationship. Then here were all these good-looking women and as the host, of course I had to pay attention to them . . ." Here Adrian smiled and held out his hands helplessly.

"You know how it is."

"Not really," replied Mickey dryly, thinking, charm, looks and talent, but what an ass. And he was the last one to see the blonde alive. And from the Burleigh woman's statement, they had argued. There were three possible scenarios here: Roxanne jumped, fell, or was pushed over the cliff. A woman who was wealthy, good-looking and possibly in love was an unlikely suicide, she thought. Petty jealousy would hardly drive her to that. A drunken partygoer might have lost her balance and fallen.

An officer had cordoned off the area and would comb the scene for clues. Police lights had been set up around the pergola, casting an eerie brilliance down the side of the rough, eroding cliff. Mickey watched the medical examiner meticulously chronicling every detail regarding the body.

There was no blood, but the weirdly bent neck and rolled-back eyes nonetheless were gruesome. The woman's aqua gown, ripped in the tumble down the cliff, exposed legs smudged with dirt and scratched from the sharp weeds growing in the cliff's crevices. Her left arm, obviously broken, was angled awkwardly away from her body, bent back at the elbow in a grotesque final wave.

Her hair, already mottled with damp sand, splayed around her head.

Could she have been pushed? Mickey wondered. Okay, Adrian was the last person known to be with Roxanne, but he claimed he left her, alive and tipsy, at the gazebo. Had someone else been there after Adrian left? Neighbors would have to be questioned, in case they saw something. Nosy neighbors could be a blessing.

Mickey's thoughts returned to Adrian. He passed off the presence of all the women at his house as normal. Just one of his regular "thank you" parties for good customers, one of their perks for investing in his custom jewelry. Still, there was something odd. Dana Burleigh had been very uneasy when she was questioned. She referred to "angry words" between Roxanne and Adrian. Mickey would definitely have to spend more time questioning that chauvinist.

LIGHTS BLAZED FROM THE WINDOWS of Adrian's home. Inside, the mood was anything but festive. The women sat in small groups, their expressions strained as they waited for their interview with Chief Brooks. Conversation was intermittent. "I just can't believe she's gone" was repeated over and over as they processed the shock of Roxy's death. In the study, doors shut, Mickey Brooks was questioning Dana Burleigh. Mickey sat behind Adrian's mahogany desk, with Dana facing her, in a leather wing chair.

"Mrs. Burleigh, what was Ms. Reynolds' mood when you last saw her? Can you go over that encounter in the bathroom again, as accurately as possible?"

Dana shifted uncomfortably. Fatigue was setting in. The conversation with Roxy seemed to have taken place light years ago.

"She—she was standing by the Chinese table in the hall drinking champagne. All of a sudden she dashed into the bathroom. I thought she might be sick, so I followed her. She said she was fine, but she seemed tense and edgy. When I brought up Adrian's charity, she just snapped. I sensed a lot of hostility from her."

"Adrian's charity? " asked Mickey. "What's that about?"

Dana paused. Although she was the newcomer, she was aware that Adrian had cautioned the members not to say too much about the Suchin Society. Membership was by his invitation only, he said, and he didn't want to alienate anyone who wasn't invited to the inner circle.

Dana thought about her husband and decided to omit any mention of the bonus jewelry.

"The women at the party tonight are all part of a group that supports Adrian's effort to establish an orphanage in Thailand. He has great plans to help the disadvantaged in that part of the world."

Mickey repressed her skepticism. Adrian—a philanthropist? Odd, I wouldn't have pegged him as anything but a womanizing opportunist—and a great designer. Interesting.

"You said Ms. Reynolds became hostile when you spoke about the orphanage. Explain what you mean."

"Well, she said that we'd all contributed a lot of money to this project and all she'd seen was a fancy brochure to show for it. I guess she thought, I don't know, that the orphanage should have been built by now. That's when I saw Adrian standing by the door. He looked angry. He came in and grabbed Roxy's shoulder."

"Grabbed? You mean he used force?" asked Mickey.

"I thought he was a little rough," replied Dana. "He obviously wanted her out of there. He said she'd had too much to drink and she should get some fresh air."

"Do you know Mr. Ferrante well?" asked Mickey.

"We've had a business relationship for several years, but do I know him personally? Not really. This was the first party of his I'd been to."

And likely to be my last, she thought. Once John got wind of tonight's drama.

"And you'd just met Ms. Reynolds, is that right? Were you aware of any personal relationship between Ms. Reynolds and Mr. Ferrante?"

"Everyone at the party knew they'd been together on the yacht. Two attractive, single people. Sure, I thought they had something going."

"Okay, thank you Mrs. Burleigh. That's all for now, but we'll want you to stay on at the Inn at least another day or so."

Mickey opened the study door for Dana and motioned for Adrian. Adrian was sitting close to a red-haired woman, her hand in his, speaking to her in a low voice. "Hang on, Maureen," Mickey heard him say. "Everything's going to be fine."

Adrian made his way to the study door. Frowning, he said," I trust this won't take long."

Mickey, smiling faintly, raised her eyebrows. Adrian headed toward his desk, then realized that the police chief's papers were spread all over the desktop.

Mickey stepped smoothly behind the desk and inclined her head toward the wing chair. "If you don't mind, Adrian?"

Adrian's stare could have frozen a chilidog. "Not at all," he replied tersely.

He sat quickly, crossing his legs. Mickey noted the well-tailored trousers, the fashionable Italian leather loafers, and thought—a man who enjoys spending money. This house, the yacht, travel—could he really afford all this on his income from the jewelry business?

Moving quickly through the routine questions, Mickey asked Adrian what he heard Roxanne say to Dana in the bathroom.

"Nothing," Adrian answered. "I was passing by, looked in, and Roxy was weaving around, looking out of it. I thought she needed some air. I led her out to the gazebo."

"Did you grab her shoulder?" Mickey asked.

"Grab? No, why would I grab my guest?" I just took her arm and helped her steady herself. She was stumbling."

"Then you heard nothing Ms. Reynolds said about your charity?"

Adrian's eyes narrowed. "What do you mean?"

"You presented this party as a routine thank-you to good customers. It seems to be something more. Mrs. Burleigh indicated that this group was contributing funds for an orphanage in Thailand. She said Ms. Reynolds was upset that the building was going so slowly, and that Ms. Reynolds became very angry and questioned your integrity."

"Ridiculous," Adrian snapped. "Roxy was a hundred percent behind the orphanage. She knew that we were about to break ground. She had faith in the project. Mrs. Burleigh must have misunderstood. This charity is a very private matter to me—I don't want to be tapped for money by every would-be do-gooder in town. But if you want to see my prospectus, I'd be happy to show it to you."

"Not right now," answered Mickey. "Right now I'm more interested in what went on between you and Ms. Reynolds on the cliff. Let's go through it again."

She led Adrian through a series of questions, finally concentrating on Roxanne's state of mind on the trip up the coast, as well as at the party and on the bluff.

"Anything to make you think she might do away with herself?"

Adrian pursed his lips, considered and finally replied. "No. She was not in that frame of mind at all. She was relaxed and happy on the Dragonfly. We had fun together, but she knew it was nothing serious. I guess she got tanked, felt a little possessive, and couldn't handle it, that's all. I shouldn't have left her out there alone. God, I blame myself."

Mickey thought, I seriously doubt that guilt will last beyond a good night's sleep. Come to think about it, there were a lot of doubts to contend with. She gathered her papers and prepared to leave, done for the night. "Stay in town, Adrian," she cautioned. "We'll need some more time with you and the ladies."

ALONE IN THE STUDY, Adrian pulled out his cell phone and scrolled until he reached the entry for Enrique Golden. They needed to talk.

Eight

Walking back to the hotel, Karin decided she'd check out early and catch the first available flight to LA. There was no sense hanging around Capitola another night. She knew she needed to touch base with Detective Ishiguro anyway.

The San Jose airport would be pretty empty at 10 on a Friday night. There wouldn't be a problem getting home at this hour. Karin got to the Southwest desk and confirmed a seat on the 11:30 flight to LAX. She cleared security, grabbed a decaf latte and settled into Gate A2 waiting area.

She wasn't looking forward to going home. Now that she'd been away for a couple of days, Karin realized she'd have to move out of the cottage she had shared with Mark. She'd never feel comfortable there again. It was a shame because she loved the little house. It had been her home for the past three years, even before Mark moved in. Her aunt owned the place; otherwise she'd never be able to afford it. But now, everything she loved about it before—the walking neighborhood with its eccentric cottages and charming gardens meandering along the canal— seemed foreign. It was all about fun. Everybody had some sort of boat tied to a wooden dock, all painted in riotous colors depending on the owner's artistic whim. The romantic atmosphere had always felt like "Wind in the Willows" to her. Their place faced the Grand Canal and although she never used her aunt's red canoe, she'd always fantasized about a sunset ride with Mark.

That, she realized, would never happen now. She needed to get used to life without him. He'd been the perfect partner, encouraging her independence while making sure she always felt protected. Mark's life was separate from hers, but she liked it that way. The only thing that mattered was when they got together they were perfectly in sync.

Now her trip to Capitola had given the perspective she needed to face the future honestly. She'd never know if their relationship could have led to something permanent. Looking back, she thought it could have worked.

Taking a deep breath, she rolled her shoulders back. It was too late at night to think about things like this. To pass the time, she took out her camera and flipped back through the photos she'd taken overlooking Capitola and the wharf. These digital cameras made it so easy.

A couple of shots were too dark. With a click, she deleted them. The others were pretty good. Maybe she'd finally get that photo album together. She had many shots from childhood visits to Capitola with images of her swimming in the lagoon and standing on the beach, tangled in seaweed as if it were a queen's robe. Photos of her and Jennie with their mom showed them sitting under a striped canvas umbrella eating those chopped olive sandwiches that Mom always made.

Clicking the "back" arrow, Karin accidentally went too far. She brought the camera closer, staring at the image in the front of her. She hadn't taken this one. What was it? She clicked "back" again and again. More of the same appeared: a Thank You Box from Golden Catering. Who took these? The date on the lens showed 8/17. Karin thought back. It didn't take long for the memory to appear, and with it a cold rock in her stomach. It was the day Mark had been killed.

Judging from the countertops, these photos had been taken in the prep kitchen at Golden Catering. She'd been in the kitchen early that day setting up for the Bel Air party. Mark had been with her, just hanging out while she finished some last-minute details. He was getting ready to take off for an audition. He wasn't even supposed to be there. Company rules. Surveillance cameras were checked often. If you're not punched in, don't let the Goldens catch you in the building.

Mark must've taken the camera out of my tote bag and snapped these pictures, she thought. But why? The box lay open, but empty. It had the jewel-encrusted top, this one in various semi-precious green stones arranged to look like ferns. Inside, the hand-painted velvet looked like lush forest moss. All the boxes were works of art, some more exquisite than others, depending on the client and how much money they spent with Golden Catering.

Karin glanced at the last photo. The floor of the box had been lifted and lay ajar. It looked like someone had been working on it and stopped mid-job. What was this all about? Karin racked her brain to figure out why Mark would take these pictures. Maybe he was just bored. That was probably it. He'd seen her camera in her purse and could never resist taking pictures of beautiful things.

The loudspeaker startled her, announcing flight 62 to LA. She turned off the camera, gathered her bags and boarded. It would be 1 a.m. by the time she made it home. She couldn't wait to take a hot bath and crash. She'd check in with Georgia and Det. Ishiguro in the morning.

Los ANGELES SEEMED BALMY compared to the foggy night in Capitola. Karin drove home thinking about the photos. She slid her key in the lock and opened the front door a crack, turning to get her luggage. As she bent down, the door flew open and hit the wall with a bang. Looking up in shock, she could see through her dark living room to the other side. The curtains to French doors that led out to the canal were swaying slightly, as if in the breeze. That's weird, she thought, I wouldn't have left those doors …

In a matter of seconds, her fight or flight reflex took over. Stepping in, she felt a chill, but the room was the same temperature as outside. Her eyes scanned, but nothing seemed out of place. She slowly felt in her purse for the cell phone. As she did, a hand reached from behind and grasped the back of her neck. Karin's head was snapped back with a velocity that threw her against the wall. Her neck made a sickening crack. She fell forward, landing on her purse.

From the floor she could see only his back. He was kneeling down going through her suitcase. She could tell she'd been out for a while because sweaters and pants were everywhere. He was slashing the sides of the suitcase with a small knife. Her wrists were duct taped behind her back, and she could taste blood. She closed her eyes and lay still.

The man was slight and wore an iridescent blue sharkskin suit, the kind made to order in Hong Kong. His straight dark hair was tied in a long thin ponytail at the back of his neck. The earring in one ear was a black cross. His shoes matched his suit perfectly and the tattoo just under his collar looked like a dragon's tail. He'd been going through her things with an experienced hand and, having found nothing, suddenly turned to her.

She had to be convincing. She couldn't let him know she was conscious. It wouldn't be hard; her head felt like it was detached. He stood, grabbed Karin's hairdryer. It came down on her skull with one crashing blow at ear level.

THE SUN WAS NEARLY UP when she finally regained consciousness. She'd come to occasionally, but slipped back each time. Now, she'd have to figure out a way to free her hands and get help. Her head stuck to the carpet. It took her a minute to realize it was dried blood. Pain pierced her neck. Each time she tried to move, a wave of nausea struck.

She looked back and saw her purse. It was open, not far from her hip. She tried to move to reach her cell phone and whimpered in pain. Grasping the phone with her taped hands she felt for the "0" and began to push down just as the phone rang.

Nine

The morning of August 25

5:30 A.M.: LIEUTENANT DETECTIVE Dan Ishiguro's hand shot out to silence his radio alarm.

He tuned in the local news station, swung his legs to the floor and crossed the hall into the tiny white cubicle of a kitchen. He filled a sleek automatic Braun water pot and glanced out the window toward the Hollywood hills.

He took a moment to enjoy the dawning sun that sent pink rays of light through neighboring trees and into a neat dark rectangle of green lawn highlighting the red and pink hibiscus blooms around the edge of the backyard.

"It's worth every penny I'm paying that neighbor kid Jay to keep the yard green and tidy," he murmured, as he replaced the pot on the heating unit at the back of a blue tiled countertop.

He reached up, grabbed a tin of sardines, two rice cakes and a tea bag from the cupboard. In one efficient movement, he set them out on the small table in the corner, turned on his heel, looked at the round-faced clock on the wall and returned to the bedroom. "Only two and a half minutes prep—new record," he mused, lowering his lean tight body to the khaki colored cotton rug to begin his morning push-ups.

The early morning newscaster was announcing a few foul-ups on the LA basin's commute. Slow for a midweek morning. He finished his exercises.

Heading to the shower, he caught his reflection in the mirror. He smoothed his neatly cropped hair. Man, he thought, I'm looking more and more like my Dad.

Poor Mom, so lonely these years since Dad died. Only 58, too young. Running his own landscaping business robbed him of his later years. Mrs. Ishiguro was so proud of her son.

A photo of Dan in full uniform commanded the central spot on her bureau.

After his shower, he stopped to punch up his computer. "Better check the e-mail," he mumbled.

Toweling off, he looked over the e-mail. "Damn spam! Hell, I don't need Viagra. I just need to meet women who don't view me with a suspicious eye as soon as they hear I'm with LAPD." A familiar thud on the front porch announced the morning Times.

Ishiguru shook out the front page, laid a sardine across a rice cake, munched, then sipped his tea.

The Times' top headline hooked his attention. "Chicago Socialite found dead on Capitola Beach."

He read further.

"Hmm . . . Dana Burleigh. Hmm . . . LA's own Dana Burleigh, alone . . . without John . . . in Capitola . . . nice little town. Hmm . . . at a party . . ." Ishiguro coughed, then called up his internal data chart.

"Capitola . . . a party . . . hmm . . . Karin Blake . . .wasn't that where she was going to do that catering job . . . that other catering job . . . boyfriend . . . murdered . . . hmm . . . interesting."

Ishiguro forgot his morning breakfast. He carefully reread the article. He took out his palm pilot, made a few notes.

"Better give Blake a call . . ."

*　　*　　*

Ishiguro's call to Karin resulted in a long ring, then what sounded like a couple of muffled cries for help before the line went dead. He tried again, but got no answer.

In his '99 Toyota Celica, he threaded his way down Sawtelle Boulevard parallel to the 405. At this time in the morning, he could make better time on the street rather than getting trapped on the freeway by an unforeseen pileup. He turned right at Venice Boulevard and headed toward the beach.

Ishiguro parked down the alley at the end of Virginia Canal Court and grumbled, helluva of a place to find parking. He took a minute to look around, then strode down the walkway along the canal to the third house from the corner. It was dwarfed by the gentrified places along the canal, remodels and new construction that had changed the run-down historical area to an upscale posh beach enclave in the last twenty years. Karin Blake's house dated from a former time, when clapboard cottages lined the old Venice canals.

He mused on how Karin could afford to live here. If she owned it, the ground under the old place must be worth a fortune. She had looked like she could use the scratch. Interesting . . .

The glass-paneled front door was locked. Calling out, he pressed the doorbell. He thought he heard sounds inside. Sheer-curtained windows in the door obscured his view. He was sure he heard a cry. He called again and listened. He pushed through overgrown shrubs around the side of the house. A French door stood wide open.

Cautiously he drew out his gun and stepped into the dining room.

"Karin?" He checked the living room. What the hell had gone on here? Chairs were tumbled about. Clothes were strewn around, emptied from a suitcase that lay slashed on the floor at the edge of the living room. Between a glass-top coffee table and a leather couch, Karin lay groaning and dazed. He leaned directly over her left ear and called her name several times. She was curled in a fetal position, her arms twisted behind her back. Blood glistened on her spiky black hair and stained a cheap oriental throw rug under her head. Her eyes opened, acknowledged him then fluttered shut again. She lay shivering and began to cry.

"Karin. It's okay. It's Ishiguro."

Replacing his gun, he pulled his cell-phone from its holster on his belt and dialed 911.

He picked his way to the bedroom, grabbed a comforter and returned to cover her. Then he noticed the duct tape around her wrists. Carefully, with his Swiss knife, he cut and removed the tape. He set it aside in an evidence envelope. He checked her pulse, then began to rub her hands and wrists.

"Karin, tell me. What happened?"

"Water . . . I need some water," she whispered.

"Okay, but just a little. We've got to get someone to look at that wound. Did you surprise someone?"

She started to nod, then groaned again.

"It's okay. Just stay still. I'll get you some water."

Ishiguro made his way to the kitchen, observing the chaos. He pulled out his cell phone, reported to headquarters and called for backup. As he turned the faucet, he could hear sirens.

"The paramedics are on top of things this morning," he thought.

KARIN PROTESTED going to the hospital. Verbally she put up a good fight; physically she was no match for the four strong, young, calm paramedics.

"I'll be along to see you, as soon as I'm through here, Karin," Ishiguro reassured her. "There's a lot to check out yet."

"My purse, where's my purse," she murmured. "He took it . . . he took it." Karin's voice trailed off to a whisper.

One of the paramedics handed Karin her purse. "We found it on the floor beside you. Yeah, and here's your cell phone, too."

" He took it," she said again.

"Hey, wait a minute." Ishiguro raced to the door where Karin lay on the gurney. He leaned over her. "What did he take?"

"My camera."

She closed her eyes.

Ishiguro checked her purse. No camera, but her wallet was still there. He turned to the paramedics. "Go ahead. Assure her I'll be along soon."

ISHIGURO NOTED IT WAS 8:30 by the time he checked at the ER desk of the Daniel Freeman Marina Hospital. Dr. Bruce Jeffries came out to discuss Karin's case: contusions on the left side of the head above the ear, whiplash and bruised ribs. He pointed out she was suffering from dehydration, lack of nutrition and, probably, sleep.

"Somebody worked her over pretty good. A good meal and a couple days' rest will help the most. She has a small frame, but remarkable strength. You can go in and see her if you like."

"Thanks Doc! What do you think caused the wound to the head?"

"I don't know, but something circular in shape. It hit initially then must've shattered. It made several surface wounds causing some bleeding. It wasn't a heavy object luckily, or it could have been fatal at that particular place."

ISHIGURO PEEKED in to find Karin eating a hearty breakfast of bacon, eggs, toast and fruit. Dark circles surrounded her eyes. Bruises darkened her left jaw. A bandage covered the left side of her head at a rakish angle. She looked like a waif out of Oliver Twist.

Ishiguro laughed.

"Think I'm your early morning entertainment? I can't chew without my whole face feeling like someone hit me with a bat. I feel like shit! When can I go home?"

"We're working on that. I'm sorry I laughed, but I've never seen anyone so beat up look so cute!"

"Well, one good thing just happened. I can stop worrying about my bill here. I called Enrique Golden to tell him what happened and that I was back. He told me not to worry about anything. Since I was working for them, they would cover everything. Only he told me not to tell Georgia. She doesn't feel exactly the same as he does about the working poor. He's really a good guy at heart. He said Workers Comp should cover everything. That he'll work it out."

Ishiguro blinked, then slowly smiled. "That's great. Nice to work for someone like that." This case was getting more interesting by the minute, he thought.

"Karin, the doctor wanted more tests, so try to get some sleep between nurses drawing blood, X-rays, that sort of thing. I'll come back in a couple of hours. They'll probably release you by then. We'll go someplace we can talk. I want to hear all the details, but you need your head clear . . . okay?"

Karin smiled, pushed the tray away and slid slowly back in bed. By the time Ishiguro glanced back from the door, her eyes were closed and she already was out of it.

THE FORENSICS CREW at Karin's house was just packing up when Ishiguro called.

"Yeah, Dan. Just about through here. We found a hair dryer under the couch that appears to be the weapon. It's cracked and has blood on it. Good thing the guy didn't use his knife. He sure used it on the overnight bag. Some valuable silver antique pieces were untouched on the dining room buffet, too. This guy was after something specific. This was no burglary. No fingerprints on the weapon, but a smudged set on the French door. That's all for now, Dan.

"Oh, yeah," the contact added. "Some gal across the canal got up around two in the morning to take a pee. She thought she heard someone climb into a boat in the canal. Sergeant Rush talked to her. He took the report before he left for headquarters. She was pretty upset, says she hid under the covers and didn't sleep another wink. She doesn't sleep so good since the murder there. That's about all I can report now. Catch ya' later. Dan."

"Thanks, Jake. I'll check with Rush."

Ishiguro put in a call to the Capitola Police. The Chief was unavailable. He left a message. He glanced at his watch—9 o'clock. It felt like noon. He had a couple of hours before he needed to pick up Karin. He called Rush then headed for the woman's house across the canal. It would pay to check out the area.

Miss Ivy Curtis ran long tapering fingers tipped with flame-red lacquer up her temples into thick dark hair streaked with gray. Slowly, she drew her arms down, hugging herself across an ample bosom loosely covered by a faded pink terrycloth robe. "This has been the worst summer of my life." She sighed heavily. She began to recount her sleepless nights, her inability to concentrate or work, her loss of appetite.

"Excuse me, Miss Curtis. Could you tell me exactly what you heard last night? If you focus carefully, you'll have better recall. We all remember things better if we think of a particular moment. It's hard to remember what you've done this summer in detail, but I'll bet you remember every moment of last night."

He gave her his most winning smile. He held up his pencil and a small, lined tablet at the ready to receive her every word. "Now, what time would you say it was?"

"Something woke me up," she said. "I lay there trying to rouse myself to go to the bathroom. I remember I looked at the clock on my nightstand and it was about twenty minutes to two. Then just when I was getting back in bed, I distinctly heard someone in the canal climb into a boat. It sort of echoes out there. I looked out the bedroom window, but it was very dark. I couldn't see a thing. I watched for a bit. Then I went back to bed and listened. I thought I heard the swish of oars, then a bump down toward the end of the canal. I pulled the covers over my head and listened. I didn't close my eyes all night."

Mrs. Curtis had been gazing off, recalling the night noises. Suddenly frowning, she turned on him.

"This is terrible," she continued. "Can you imagine what this is doing to our property values here? I certainly hope you police will have some protection for our neighborhood. What's being done to catch the murderer?"

Ishiguro snapped his tablet shut, slid the pencil into his pocket, bowed slightly, handed her his card and backed away.

"We'll be in touch. You've been a terrific help, Miss Curtis." He quickly walked down the canal, looking at boats tied up along the way. When he reached the bridge, he noticed a small red canoe drawn up, but not tied, under the bridge by steps leading to the walkway. He dialed Jake to come back.

"Give that boat a thorough going over. This may give us a break, a break we need."

About 11:30, Ishiguro got the okay to sign Karin out of the hospital. After her wheelchair ride to the exit, he brought his car around to the curb. Karin didn't look too steady yet, Ishiguro thought, as he eased her into the passenger's side of his Celica. He slid into the driver's side, paused before starting the car, and asked, "How about lunch? I spotted a Mexican joint about a block from your place. Do you know it? Ever go there? Would you recommend it? Do you feel up to it?"

Suddenly, his voice sounded too loud, too forced, to his own ear. She had the damnedest effect on him.

He didn't want to go back to her place before he had a chance to question her. He was sure she would be overwhelmed when she saw the mess. He needed to have her focus.

Karin turned slowly, searching his dark eyes for a moment. She wasn't hungry, but didn't want to go home. "Yes, Chico's, that sounds good. It's sorta my home away from home actually."

She felt warmed by this guy. Underneath that efficient, cool exterior she sensed real heart. She hadn't met many of those types lately.

"They do a mean super-burrito. Yeah, that would be great!"

Ishiguro drove smoothly out of the parking lot, turned right and connected with Lincoln Boulevard. He headed north to Washington Boulevard, then turned left down to Ocean Avenue just east of the canals. Chico's lit up the corner. It was an old stucco building that had been painted with varying horizontal bands of yellow orange, red-orange and more yellow. A large "Chico's" sign cut a swath above the green door. Ishiguro parked, and they entered between phony coconut trees guarding either side of the door.

"Hey Chiquita! Where you been? What happened to you?"

A heavy-set Latino with a broad flat face leaned across a bar looking concerned.

"Hi Raphael! I ran into a bad-ass man. But this is a nice man. Meet Detective Ishiguro."

Karin waved and walked toward the back of the dark room. She paused at a double door that led into a patio. "Out here, detective Dan."

"Hey man, nice to meetcha!" Raphael enclosed Ishiguro's hand in a large damp paw. "Take good care of her. She's havin' some bad karma lately, man. She don't deserve it neither."

Karin smiled thinly at her old friend. "All those years of kick boxing didn't do me a damned bit of good. Big-time bummer."

"You're a kick boxer?" Ishiguro eyed her in disbelief.

"Yeah, I've done it for years. Even won awards."

Hmm, Dan thought. I wouldn't want to be at the end of her foot . . . or would I . . .

Raphael picked up two menus and followed them to a table in the covered patio.

"Two of your super burritos, Raphael." Karin turned toward Ishiguro. "Sorry, I hope that's alright? I just assumed you'd like to try the house special, carne asada?"

"That's exactly what I'd like." Ishiguro smiled.

"How I'd love an icy cold Pacifico, but the doctor ordered absolutely no alcohol for a while. How about a vanilla horchata?"

"Horchata? What's that?"

"Something to cool the spice, soothe the tummy," she said.

"Sounds good. I'll try it."

The atmosphere was right, friendly. It was a good time to talk.

His cell phone rang, breaking the mood.

"Dan Ishiguro here. Who? Oh, yes, I did call earlier . . . excuse me a moment."

He slid out of his seat. "It's important, Karin. Be back shortly."

TEN MINUTES LATER, Ishiguro was back with a scowl.

"Let's order these burritos to go. I just talked to the chief of police in Capitola, Karin. Did you know a Mrs. Roxanne Reynolds, a guest at Adrian Ferrante's party last night?" He watched Karin's reaction intently.

"Roxanne Reynolds?" she paused. "No, I barely saw any of the guests. I'm supposed to be invisible at Georgia's parties, ya know. Georgia has always commended me for my unobtrusive presence," Karin noted ironically. "Why? I did see Dana Burleigh, the congressman's wife, being pulled along the sidewalk by her damn dog. She and her insufferable, inseparable dog have been at several of Georgia's parties in LA. We just catered one last month. In Capitola, I saw her walking to the party about 8 o'clock. Why? What happened?"

"Roxanne Reynolds was found dead at the bottom of the cliff below the Ferrante property. Mrs. Burleigh's dog found her."

"Oh no. Oh my God! Not another murder!" Fierce anxiety started in the pit of her stomach and spread through her body. She froze. She couldn't think.

Dan observed her reaction, then continued, "The Capitola police chief wants you back there as soon as possible, and she wants me with you. She already confirmed it with my office. She assured me you can rest up there, but she made it clear, you are to be present when . . ."

Wearily, Karin heaved a sigh of resignation and looked up. "You don't believe I had anything to do with Mark's murder, let alone what happened there, do you?"

She wasn't going with him until she had an answer.

Ishiguro reached over, squeezed her hand and gave her a comforting smile.

Then he called, "Hey, Raphael, wrap these to go, would ya, please?"

He turned back to Karin. "I'm collecting some interesting pieces to this puzzle. So far, I'm on your side." He reached to help her up.

Was that an answer? Enigmatic . . . that's the word for him, she thought.

She felt vulnerable. This was making her miss Mark more than ever. Well, thanks to Dan, she did feel protected.

Karin slid into the warm, buttery leather car seat and leaned back on the headrest as Ishiguro closed the passenger door.

She sighed. She was tired, and she hurt all over. She felt like shit.

He got into the driver's seat and paused after putting his keys in the ignition. He glanced at her sloping shoulders and limp body.

"Karin, I have a proposal. We need to get a flight to San Jose later this afternoon. In the meantime, I've got some work to do before we go. Why not pick up a few things at your place, enough for a couple of days. We'll go back to my house. You can rest, sleep, take a shower, whatever . . . while I go to the office. Your place is a mess. I don't think you're in any mood to clean house right now. Right? Besides, I'm not sure forensics finished checking it out. How does that sound?"

"Sounds like heaven. Some food, a bath and a long nap before I have to face Capitola again would be great."

God, it was nice to be taken care of by someone who seemed to understand, she thought.

Her nerves had felt like jangled wires for so long. Suddenly, a calming peace infused her muscles and her mind.

KARIN AWAKENED refreshed—achy, but refreshed—for the first time in days. Nothing like a burrito, a hot shower and a long nap. She stretched. She looked around. It took a moment to realize where she was. She loved the basic beige, wheat and white colors that dominated the room. There was a simple efficiency to Dan's house. She dressed hastily. Pulling on her khakis and a black pullover, she thought, I blend in nicely here. She just had time to put on some makeup and gingerly run her fingers through her hair.

"Ouch," she winced.

She heard a car door slam in the driveway then Ishiguro's key in the door, and she felt a surge of optimism.

"Wow! What a difference a few hours can make," Ishiguro appraised her transformation.

Karin liked what she saw in his eyes.

They barely caught a 5:15 Southwest flight for San Jose. Karin couldn't stop talking. During the flight, she recounted every detail she could remember from the previous night, and went back over things she remembered about the past few months.

For the first time in weeks she felt she was really alive. She was determined to help bring together all the bits and pieces from her memory and tie them in with Summer and Margo's stories. There had to be a common thread to explain the madness that had begun with Mark's death.

Now, with Dan to count on, she could hardly wait to get back to Summer and Margo.

"You've suddenly become awfully thoughtful."

Dan smiled at Karin. I worried for nothing, he thought. Rather than having to interrogate her, she'd opened up like a sluice box, but surprisingly, as they neared Capitola she'd become pensive and quiet.

It was 7:15 when Dan steered the rental car off Highway 1 onto the Capitola off-ramp.

Ten

The morning of August 25
Silverlake, Los Angeles

7:30 A.M.: GEORGIA GOLDEN decided to have a simple breakfast in the atrium—coffee, a Morning Bun and of course, the morning paper. She unfolded the Times and gasped. "Dana Burleigh!" Her company had catered the Burleighs' big party just last month.

"And Buddy! That little pest."

"Rick! Rick! Come here. At once!" she called to her husband. Enrique Golden appeared from his bathroom, his face lathered, ready for his favorite time, the morning shave.

"Read this headline!" She shoved the paper toward him. "My God, this is Adrian's party. The one we catered last night in Capitola. And not a word from that bitch Karin Blake. I'll get her hide. Skinny little no-good . . . She's history with us, Rick."

Enrique Golden read the headline, scanned the first paragraphs, and paled.

Chicago Socialite Found Dead on Capitola Beach

Pet Dog Buddy Leads Congressman's Wife to Body

CAPITOLA, AUGUST 25—Dana Eldridge Burleigh, wife of LA Congressman John Burleigh, left a party hosted by jet-set jeweler Adrian Ferrante last night in Capitola to walk her dog, Buddy. The dog ran off and began barking.

Mrs. Burleigh found her dog, a Yorkshire Terrier, at 9 p.m. on the beach, next to the body of Roxanne Webber Reynolds, 48, of Chicago, who was identified by Ferrante. Well-known Realtor from the prominent Webber family, owners of the Chicago Whites, Mrs. Reynolds also had been a guest at the Ferrante home on the cliff directly above the site where the body was found.

The western end of the beach in this central coast resort village is crowded with sunbathers in the day, but after sunset normally is deserted, so the possibility of witnesses is slim, said Capt. Buzz Jones of the Capitola Police Department.

Mrs. Burleigh told police that she arrived at the Ferrante home around 8 p.m. with Buddy. Shortly before dinner, she took the dog down the old wooden steps to the beach for a short walk, and let him off the leash. "He ran off down the beach," she said, "and then I heard him barking frantically." Accompanied by another party guest, Charlotte Gallatin of Atlanta, GA, Mrs. Burleigh located her dog and made the grim discovery.

Ferrante, the third generation of prestigious Capitola jewelers, identified Mrs. Reynolds as one of his ten guests, friends from throughout the country who share a common interest in jewelry. All are female. A guest list has been provided to the Capitola PD. All guests were retained for questioning last night at the Ferrante mansion.

Congressman Burleigh was unavailable for comment, according to an aide reached at his downtown Los Angeles office.

Capitola Police Chief Mickey Brooks confirmed the investigation will be conducted in her jurisdiction.

Downtown Los Angeles

8 A.M. CONGRESSMAN John Burleigh slammed his office door and stomped to the desk, ignoring the seventeenth-story view of City Hall. "Damn her. Damn that damn dog. Damn Adrian Ferrante. Damn the Times."

Burleigh's aide, James Evans, set an issue of the morning LA Times on his desk and stepped into the Congressman's office. "Bad news. I'm sorry sir. What would you like me to do?"

"Get us a couple of tickets to San Jose, pronto. You and I are going north to kick some ass," Burleigh growled.

The congressman's size magnified his gruff personality.

At six-foot, four and weighing nearly 260, the former prosecutor intimidated strangers more readily than befriending them. Connections and years of tough convictions, not cozy campaign promises, clinched his elections.

Pounding his way to the outer office, he nearly upset a potted palm.

He stared in disbelief at the Times front page and the photo of him and his wife from last year's campaign. Crooked into her right arm, was Buddy. He hated that dog.

Silverlake, Los Angeles

8:30 A.M. AS IF ON A REGULAR morning run, Enrique Golden, freshly shaved and in his Armani jogging pants and tee, paced himself.

Finally out of sight of the house, he turned off course and sprinted toward Silverlake Park.

A tall, slender figure stepped from behind a weeping willow along the lake to approach the jogger. Enrique followed the young man into the shade.

"Well?" Enrique's right hand slid into his pants pocket.

"Bingo," came the reply, with a slightly foreign inflection.

"And?" Enrique was shifting his weight from foot to running-shoed foot.

The contact held out a digital camera. "They're loaded on the card. See for yourself."

The screen flicked on. Enrique inspected a series of photographs taken in the kitchen at Golden Catering.

"How many are there?" he asked.

"Seven."

"That should do it. Good work, Ratsami. You do credit to the Naris name. So, give me the memory card out of the camera."

He took the card.

"You'll hear from me again."

Enrique pulled a roll of twenty one-hundred dollar bills from his pocket, handed it over, took the card, and headed home.

The Naris clan comes in handy, he mused as he drove. Good ole Uncle Jao. Great worker. At least

Georgia loves him. I'm just glad he knows to keep his trap shut about that low-life nephew of his.

At home, the gold Porsche was in the first garage. Fortunately, Enrique had remembered his car keys. Georgia would never see him.

He reached in the trunk for his laptop, inserted the card and pulled a wool blanket over the computer. Quietly, he clicked it shut, closed the trunk and jogged back out to the path and up to the atrium door.

Georgia folded the paper, glared at her husband and stated, "I'm going to Capitola." Enrique's face was obscured as he bent to untie his running shoes. He grunted, "I'd better go, too."

Eleven

Enrique Golden shoved his wife's bag in the overhead, then eased in his own black bag with his laptop.

Georgia snapped open her lavender Borkin, reached for a Valium and shut her bag with vehemence. The flight attendant, leggy in her pleated slacks, bent over Enrique and offered Georgia a warm towel. Clearly the woman needed to be calmed; if it were the Fourth of July, she'd be a Roman candle.

"Champagne?" The flight attendant offered. "Or water, perhaps? Perrier? Our pastry today is strawberry cream puff."

"Nothing," Georgia replied abruptly.

Enrique smiled radiantly from his leather seat.

"Perrier would be dandy, my dear. And yes on the snack."

Georgia noticed a slight tremor in his hand as he reached for the flight magazine. It would be a long hour to San Jose.

Enrique stiffened to push his chair back, shut his eyes. Take-off was imminent, he hoped. The drive to the airport had been hell with the bitch talking non-stop all the way, then accusing him … him! … of taking the wrong turn. Well, he'd shut her up good back there at valet parking. She's so edgy lately … If she only knew how bad things could get for them. Fortunately, he wasn't in it alone. He had to manage Adrian, not let him blab. And the cops! How much did they know? How the hell did that broad go over Adrian's cliff?

"Honey, let's not fight." Georgia said softly. "Let's just enjoy this little getaway. Everything will be fine."

"We'll see," Enrique grumbled, eyes still shut. He thought of the memory card with its damning evidence, safe for now in his laptop. He'd have to destroy the card, and soon.

Crystal flutes of sparkling water arrived, and two perfect pastries, swans afloat in little seas of strawberry coulis.

"I've been thinking," Georgia leaned closer and tweaked his cheek. "Maybe we need a real vacation. I've been reading about Thailand. It must be beautiful. How about it, Rick hon? The staff will run things perfectly well while we're away."

"What?" Enrique almost shouted, bolted straight in his seat and stared at her. "What did you say?"

"Thailand, darling," she purred. "You know, Bangkok, rice paddies, new food ideas for the company. It's quite the attraction, you know. I could do a little shopping. Lots of good buys. Beachside hotels. Just ten days or so. We could line up tickets online when we get to Capitola."

"You're insane," Enrique tried to ignore sweat beading on his forehead. "We can't leave LA. Losing two employees, and the fall season starting up, there's too much to do. Not for ten days. And not Thailand."

"You just don't want to go away with me," she spit back. "You'd rather slip off with some long-legged 20-year-old. I know you, you bastard."

"I don't do that and you know it," he growled back.

"Then how about all those young Asian guys you seem to attract, Mr. Z? I see things. I put two and two together. Maybe you'd rather go off for a fun weekend in San Francisco, without wifey-poo."

"Shut up, Georgia. Okay. If you want to go somewhere, we can. After this stuff in Capitola blows over, and we replace that guy Mark, and the bitch, Karin, we'll take off. Where'd you want to go, then? New York? Catch a couple of plays? Shop? Mexico? That villa you liked, Sol de-Something in San Miguel?"

He signaled for more water, glanced out at the arid landscape moving below. Forty minutes more to landing.

ENRIQUE'S BLOOD BOILED. She'd called him Mr. Z again.

He hated it when she called him that. I know she's trying to kiss ass, like it's supposed to make up for everything. I'll never forget my name's Enrique Zimmerman, he assured himself. He was proud of his family name, but when they were married, she insisted he go by Golden. The bitch, so class conscious and worried about her image. Golden Catering ruled their lives. He was proud of his Argentine roots, that his mother was a native. And proud of his father, a German who'd fled after the fall of Hitler's regime.

But there was no convincing Georgia, he thought venomously. It's always about her. He glowered.

WAITING FOR THEIR RENTAL CAR, with Georgia in the girls' room, Enrique reached for his cell and dialed a Capitola number, waited for an answer, then spoke.

"We'll be there in about an hour," he said. Then, "Shit, no. We'll go together when I get there. Right."

He shoved the phone into his jacket pocket and turned to wait for his wife.

Enrique signed for the Mercedes, wound out of the airport and headed over the coastal mountains to Santa Cruz, then down Highway 1 to Capitola. Easy listening music on the radio took care of Georgia's mouth, but an uneasiness darkened Enrique's thoughts.

How far could he trust Adrian, he asked himself. Maybe involving the jeweler was a mistake. What if Adrian had offed that broad at his party? Bad press is one thing, but bad blood in two cities . . .

He thought back to LA, that day he'd found their caterers' Thank You Box dismantled. And now the photos in his laptop.

Damn. The cops were all over that kid's murder. He'd show Adrian the photos as soon as they were alone.

Georgia shifted to look at him. As if she were reading his thoughts. "You know we're going to be called in to testify about that guy, Mark, when we're through in Capitola. I want to go anywhere but back to LA. OK?"

"What's wrong with you?" Enrique glared into the rear-view mirror. "Guilty conscience?"

If you only knew, Georgia thought.

Twelve

CHARLOTTE GALLATIN slept fitfully, despite the comfort of the king-sized pillow-top four-poster in the Inn's $500 VIP suite. She had planned to leave today, but she really didn't mind staying on. It was no big problem. Her husband, Richard, was traveling for another week, and nobody would miss her except Missy, her Siamese cat.

Last night, the policewoman told everyone at Adrian's party, including the wait staff, the kitchen help and the party guests, that they were considered material witnesses to Roxy Reynolds' death. Brooks warned, "No one has my permission to return home until further notice. Those of you who are staying at the Inn at Soquel Creek should arrange to meet me there tomorrow at five o'clock, when we will continue our interviews."

Charlotte got up, jumped in the shower and turned up the hot water. She went over the events of last night. Around eight, she, Loretta Matthews and Roxy Reynolds had taken the Inn's private limo, but because of limited parking, they were dropped off a short distance from Adrian's bluff top home. Walking single file along the narrow street, Charlotte heard Loretta, who was in front of her, muttering obscenities. Then she'd blurted out at Roxy, "Why are you circulating these filthy rumors? Telling everyone that my Jerry is involved with a tramp stripper from San Francisco?"

Not responding, Charlotte and Roxy kept on walking.

Loretta had persisted. "And spreading vicious lies about our Fresno agribusiness failing. Really. I'm not naming names, but I will kill a certain someone if she doesn't stop spreading this kind of shit."

Roxy was about to respond when they saw Adrian standing in the doorway. Loretta, now all smiles, took her host's arm. Adrian whisked her off somewhere inside. As Charlotte stopped to leave her wrap in the foyer, Roxy whispered something disturbing.

She remembered it clearly, now that Roxy was dead.

Primping in front of an ornate 15th century gilt mirror, Roxy had said, "Loretta's scumbag hubby and his trashy girl friend were with me and Adrian on his yacht over Fourth of July weekend. I'm telling the truth. We anchored in Santa Barbara and picked them up. I don't know why Loretta's pissed at me. I phoned her from the Dragonfly and told her, 'Do you know what's going on?' Well, she went berserk. After calling me a pig-faced gossip, she actually said she felt like killing me. Then she hung up. Well, she just repeated it. You heard her."

That was God's truth. Charlotte would swear it on her family Bible. She turned off the shower and felt cleansed all over.

CHARLOTTE SHUT THE TALL, carved oak door at the Inn's entrance and waited in the shade of the porte cochere until her eyes adjusted to the glare bouncing off the white stucco walls. The morning sun peeked over the red-tiled rooftop. She loved the place. Home to a San Francisco capitalist in the 1920s, the Spanish style mansion had been beautifully restored to its former glory. She crossed the courtyard and admired the antique sundial in a newly planted bed of white petunias, a reminder of her mother's summer garden in Savannah.

Charlotte had thrown a paisley scarf around her shoulders before leaving her room, but as she followed the brick walkway encircling the grounds, she started to shiver. Darn, she thought, the weather is like the people living here—unpredictable. Capitola's climate in August was nothing like Atlanta. When it got hot there, it stayed hot.

Her teal cashmere twin set and tan slacks were a peace offering from a wandering husband who always plied her with gifts instead of attention. The outfit was like him, inadequate in keeping her warm. But she would make the best of it; she always did.

As she approached the reflection pool at the edge of the grounds, she was drawn to the peaceful sound of the water bubbling from an old stone spigot that some craftsman had restored. Breathing deeply and gazing into the clear liquid, she felt herself drift into a meditative state. The stress she had been carrying for the past twelve hours disappeared; Charlotte felt revived.

Giant eucalyptus to the south of the Inn swayed in the breeze, beckoning her to join them. Her

Ferragamos with thin leather soles were the wrong shoes for this natural habitat. Eucalyptus pods strewn everywhere poked into the soles of her feet. But the discomfort was worth it. Looking up, she reflected that in a few months thick clusters of inert orange and brown Monarch butterflies would be hanging from the high branches. A small, posted sign reminded her they would be resting and feeding on the nearby milkweed before starting their annual southward flight to Mexico.

Charlotte wondered if Adrian's women would be happier if they got along like the butterflies, instead of competing with one another. She had told the police chief only last night that she thought most of them were aloof, spoiled and judgmental. She was different. Hadn't she befriended Dana Burleigh, the wife of a congressman? As a girl, Charlotte had been taught to please others—Southern manners, some would say. That must be the reason.

They had met over cocktails in Adrian's living room and laughed at some of the women's feathered, sequined frocks, appropriate for a big city party perhaps, but out of place in a beach town like Capitola. Charlotte had always liked younger people, with their fresh new ideas. After a few glasses of Pinot Noir, the conversation took an intimate turn. She amazed herself when she had revealed to Dana that her marriage of thirty years was falling apart. Somewhat embarrassed, she'd quickly turned the tables on her companion and asked, "Why have you decided to join Adrian's circle?"

Dana's answer took her by surprise.

"You really want to know my reason?" she responded. "I'll only confess it to you, Miss Charlotte. After all, you've been frank with me. John is so self-absorbed, politically driven. He assumes that our sizable gifts of money will be going to a good cause."

Then she added, "Adrian's fabulous jewelry is what really turns me on—all those gorgeous pieces he designs for us. I've loved expensive baubles all my life. I plan to buy as many as I can, without my frugal husband being the wiser."

They had giggled, and unwittingly Charlotte in turn revealed another secret. "My personal trust fund, not my husband's beer company, pays for Adrian's jewelry."

What made her confess that? The wine did it. Or, was she desperate to tell someone her troubles, instead of always listening to theirs. Being candid, especially with strangers, was a rare event in her life.

Her thoughts turned to her interview with Mickey Brooks. The chief wouldn't let up, drilling her with questions. In Charlotte's book, the chief was downright rude.

"When did you first notice the body?"

"Was anyone walking near you on the beach?"

"Come on, now, *Mrs.* Gallatin, you must have been using those eyes."

Charlotte described the impromptu beach stroll with Dana and her little dog Buddy.

Mickey had leaned over the desk. "And you saw no one? That's hard to believe, *Mrs.* Gallatin. And heard nothing unusual? Okay, describe your friend's body when you first saw it."

STUMBLING UPON ROXY'S BODY at the base of the bluff had caused Charlotte to wake up trembling every few hours that night.

She couldn't imagine anyone on top of the cliff pushing a helpless woman to her death. She closed her eyes, bowed her head, murmured a prayer for Roxy.

The pungency of the eucalyptus reminded her of the incense during all those funeral masses she'd attended. Her grandparents, aunts and uncles. Below the grove, she could hear the muffled sound of the surf as the tide pushed its way into the creek.

Then she remembered—the interview with the police chief. So put off by the chief's brusqueness, she'd neglected to mention what Roxy had whispered, about Loretta's threats to kill her. She'd better take care of that.

Her ruminations were interrupted by the fluttering of restless birds in the nearby acacia trees. Loretta! She was supposed to meet her at nine. She'd be waiting at the Inn's outdoor café, nestled between the lobby and guest bungalows edging the creek. After the police interviews last night, Loretta said she had something to tell Charlotte, but it would have to keep until they had some sleep.

She hurried past the old water tower housing the butterfly habitat interpretive center, and headed back to the Inn. The glass wedding chapel, its columned pergola covered with heritage roses, looked abandoned in the filtered sunlight. She remembered her own wedding in Savannah. Her father spared no expense in giving his only daughter a wonderful sendoff. Little did she dream then that her youthful expectations would turn out to be unfulfilled illusions.

* * *

Excited voices spilled out of the outdoor café. The aroma of freshly roasted coffee beans filled the air. She saw Loretta sitting with Sandi Weaver at an umbrella-covered table. Their outfits seemed better suited for cocktails than morning coffee. Loretta dazzled in a tight black sweater and low-rise white slacks revealing her tanned midriff. "Hi, there. Come join us," she motioned to Charlotte. Her dangling silver earrings sparkled in the sunlight. Poor Loretta, Charlotte thought, trying to put on a happy face.

"Hey," Charlotte greeted them. She signaled the waitress to bring some coffee. Loretta knew that Charlotte was a great listener. That was probably why Loretta had latched on to her. Was she also grasping at Sandi for support?

Sandi chirped, "Charlie, where ya'll been hidin'?" As she waved her left wrist, her diamond-studded platinum bracelet caught the sunlight. Sandra Weaver, or as she told everyone, Sandi with an "i" was in her late forties. With blonde hair in a boyish bob, a tan, and an unlined face, she could pass for late thirties. Her St. John shirtwaist in muted creamy yellows and short matching sweater flattered her curvaceous figure. Yesterday, Charlotte had noticed Sandi flaunting her wares before the Esplanade's male pub-crawlers.

Uncrossing perfectly tanned legs, Sandi lifted the straw from her empty bottle of Volvic water and twirled the bottle playfully on the table. "Spin the bottle anyone?" She turned to Charlotte. "We've been waitin' for you for hours, honey lamb," she exaggerated in her thick, Texas accent. "Guess you've been on your mornin' constitutional, or whatever you call it. I don't know why you do that, darlin'. You're so thin already. As soon as you finish your coffee, we're takin' off."

She pulled a wad of fives from her straw purse and slapped a few bills on the table. "My treat, ladies. No arguin' now. Meet ya'll in the lobby."

Not your treat at all, sugar, Charlotte thought. It's Daddy's oil money. That's what pays for everything you buy.

BRIGHT SUNLIGHT illuminated hidden recesses and corners of the Inn's spacious drawing room as Charlotte and her friends gathered in front of tall French doors leading to the solarium. Since they were free until five, Charlotte suggested a driving excursion around Monterey Bay to Carmel. She hoped the trip would take her mind off Roxy's death. She recommended lunch at Hotel La Playa once they'd finished shopping in Carmel's quaint shops. It would be a perfect diversion, she thought, though she wondered how many of them would be able to enjoy it.

THE GROUP IDLED AWAY the afternoon in Carmel Village and returned to the Inn with half an hour to spare before scheduled appointments with Police Chief Brooks. Charlotte showered and changed into a long, black silk skirt and a fitted white blouse. A few minutes before five, she descended the circular staircase to the "Great Hall," the high-ceilinged former living room of the historic mansion. The hall now served as the watering hole for the Inn's guests and locals alike. The place was packed. Most stood two deep at the cocktail bar. Early birds had settled in overstuffed chairs surrounding the big stone fireplace.

The manager waved from his post behind the reception desk; Charlotte returned the greeting and looked around for a place to sit. In the far corner, the piano player ran through his repertoire of Forties ballads. She hummed along to "Stormy Weather."

Elodia Verdugo, a charter member of Adrian's Society and wife of an international financier, beckoned to Charlotte from the window seat overlooking the creek. She made room for Charlotte. Elodia provided the charming accent the room needed, with her flowing dark hair, beautiful smile and a luminous green suit.

She wore a vintage Bulgari ring on her right hand, but no wedding band.

"Charlotte, how are you, querida?" she said. "Estas bien?" Her lilting Spanish reflected her South American heritage. Her brown eyes glistened in the soft light.

"I'm all right, dear, considering what we've all been through. How about you?"

"Bueno. Not bad. But I'm worried about Maureen. My suite is next to hers in the pink bungalows by the rose arbor. We had planned to swim together after lunch, but she didn't ring my room. Que pasa?"

Charlotte recalled that neither Elodia nor Maureen had joined the group for their afternoon shopping trip to Carmel.

"I called her several times, but no answer. I checked with the front desk. Nada." Elodia frowned. "You know what I think? She didn't come back with us last night after the police chief's questioning. What do you suppose happened to her?"

Maureen McCrae was the very young and very beautiful trophy wife of a successful Phoenix real estate developer. They were new money. She'd been part of Adrian's crowd for a little over a year.

"When did you last see Maureen?" Charlotte asked Elodia.

"At the party, outside on the terrace. I'm sure it was before Roxy fell, at least I think it was. I was so upset after that I couldn't think straight."

"What was Maureen doing out there?"

"Talking to Adrian. I heard her say she'd call a cab—something like that. Why would she do that? The party wasn't over and the limos were available to bring us back to the Inn. I'm worried. We mustn't lose another member." She shivered.

A COMMOTION AT THE FRONT DESK interrupted them. Capitola's police chief was in the center of a throng of people, clapping her hands for attention. Her dark blue uniform stood out in marked contrast to the colorful array of pantsuits and dresses.

Charlotte surveyed the crowd. She was surprised to see the Goldens. They weren't part of Adrian's Suchin Society. Georgia and Enrique, a couple from Southern California, owned the catering company Adrian always used. She had hired them herself for parties at Pot Belly Beach a few miles downwind from Capitola village. She occasionally rented a house there. Why were the Goldens here, she wondered.

Everyone looked up as two men, the younger carrying a bulging briefcase, descended the staircase. Charlotte recognized the older man from a recent photo in the Atlanta newspaper. He'd been pictured with his arm around baseball idol Mark McGuire during congressional investigations concerning the use of steroids. This was Dana Burleigh's husband. He was the ranking member on the House Government Relations Committee. When had he arrived in Capitola?

MICKEY BROOKS RESTED her forehead on the mahogany desk. She was halfway through her interviews with "Adrian's Army," as she was starting to call the assembly of women. To put it mildly, they were driving her crazy. That they could find Adrian a source of endless fascination—and they seemed to, to a woman—was beyond Mickey's comprehension. She started the interviews by asking for a description of the events of the party, and so far, all of the stories had jibed.

Then, turning her focus to Adrian, she'd established each woman's connection to him, and asked for an assessment of the man and his character. Watching woman after woman grow all dewy as they babbled on about their adored jeweler made Mickey want to hurl.

Well now, that's a professional attitude, she thought wryly. It'll get me nowhere fast.

To relax, she inhaled deeply through her nose, then opened her mouth and exhaled forcefully, using the ocean-sounding breath from yoga class. Yoga kept her limber as well as relaxed and, she hoped, helped her weekly golf games. Right now, it would keep her sane while she interviewed the rest of "Adrian's Army."

She rose, went to the library door. Her voice cut through the crowd's chatter. "All right, everyone," she announced. "We have more questions. Please follow me."

She called for the next interviewee.

CHARLOTTE, STILL WAITING HER TURN, glanced around again and wondered what had happened to Maureen. Why hadn't she shown up? Did she know something about Roxy Reynolds' death?

Just then, the entry door opened. Adrian Ferrante entered and turned to hold it for his female companion, Maureen McCrae. Adrian put his arm around her waist and they entered. The crowd parted as the couple moved slowly to the center of the great room. Charlotte saw a disheveled young woman still in the same gorgeous gown she'd worn the evening before. Her hair desperately needed combing and her eyes were red; she'd been crying.

Maureen appeared reluctant to let go of Adrian, Charlotte noticed. She watched Adrian deftly slide his arm down across her backside with just a hint of a pat. He stepped around her and continued on. For a moment, Maureen looked lost. She avoided eye contact with those watching her. Then she quickly made for the stairs. From the library doorway, Mickey Brook's authoritative tone froze Maureen's right foot on the first step. All eyes in the room focused on her rigid back.

"Mrs. McCrae! You have not reported in today. Be prepared for your interview in twenty minutes."

Maureen turned slowly, her tumbled red hair framing a pale expressionless face.

"I'm sorry," she said. "I'll be ready."

The expectant hush in the dining room erupted into fizzy little conversations. Maureen continued measured steps up the stairs.

Hmm, I bet that little kitten lands on all four paws in any situation, Charlotte mused.

ADRIAN BUTTONED his sport jacket as he crossed the room, headed straight for the bar, and ordered his signature Manhattan, Blanton Whiskey and imported French cherries. He took a sip, glanced with distaste at the gossiping women, and exited to the terrace.

Far below, Soquel Creek stood dark green, cloaked in thick vegetation on both sides. Willows, eucalyptus and cottonwoods merged in an overhead thicket. The dappled light created a peaceful scene complete with late summer boaters enjoying the cool, tranquil setting.

Adrian had been raised on these waters. There were many summers swimming in the lagoon and paddling up the creek to catch frogs and steelhead salmon. It wouldn't be half bad being transported back to those days right about now, he mused. Standing alone on the back deck of the Inn gave him a few moments of much-needed solitude. The last twenty-four hours had been exhausting. Just when you think everything is going fine, the bottom drops out. Roxy turned out to be a bigger pain than he'd expected. The company of these women wasn't always worth the varied perks. He'd better be more careful in his choice of associates.

Someone behind him cleared his throat. Adrian turned in surprise, but in an instant he composed himself, finishing his drink in one, big swallow. Without a word, he turned, as if to leave the terrace. He was not alone.

Enrique approached him, "Well?"

Adrian's reply was cool. "What took you so long?"

After a tentative handshake, Adrian said, "Let's not talk here. We should get over to the house. Nothing's happening here right now. The girls will probably go for dinner. Get Georgia. Let's get out of here."

It was a short walk from the Inn to Adrian's place on Aquamarine Drive. It was dinnertime in the homes perched above the creek. Pungent aromas drifted from barbecues. Someone was sautéing garlic in olive oil. As Adrian and the Goldens passed beautifully groomed tropical gardens along the steep hill, a couple boarded the red and gold funicular railway, headed for dinner near the creek, at The Shadowbrook.

AT NUMBER ONE AQUAMARINE, Adrian led them around to French doors off the veranda. The sun had nearly set, pouring the last of its golden light over the wharf below. Boats at anchor bobbed gently, seeming to bow to an impressive yacht moored alongside the wharf, Adrian's Dragonfly.

The men sat at the bar.

Georgia shrugged a fuzzy jacket over her shoulders and strolled out to the cliff. So nice up here, she thought, breathing in the sea air. Away from the oppressive smog. If only it had worked out with Adrian . . . If only . . .

She glanced over the cliff and gasped. Directly below, garish yellow police tapes glistened in the waning sunlight, flapping slightly over the sand, marking the chalked outline of a human figure.

Georgia hurried back to the house to find her husband and the man who, long ago, she'd loved.

"Adrian! How horrible. And during your very special party. Who was she? Anyone Rick and I might know? My God. So bad for you . . . where were you when she fell?"

She was on a roll; questions tumbled out like popcorn in a beachside vending machine.

"Shut up, George," Enrique muttered her nickname.

Adrian calmly set up three wine glasses.

"French?" he asked lightly, "or this latest New Zealand sauvignon blanc? I'm mad about New Zealand whites just now."

"Nothing," Georgia replied icily. "I need to freshen up."

She turned abruptly. Adrian glanced at her retreating rear and thought, not the girl she once was. Who did her colors anyway? Various shades of barf. And those fingernails. More like painted claws. Vegas gone bad, he decided. Probably the influence of her tacky husband. Definitely seedy. He continued to busy himself at the bar.

WHEN HIS WIFE WAS SAFELY out of range, Enrique turned, ignored the wine, and asked, "Did you get them out of here in time? Where are they?"

"No panic. They're in the safe at the shop. No one's seen them, not even my assistant, and if she had, she's a jewel herself. She'd never mention a thing."

"So." Enrique paused. "What about this Roxanne? Man, when I saw the Times this morning, I started to wonder why I ever got involved with you. Things are adding up bad. First our courier, Mark, gets it; and now, bang! One of your guests goes over the cliff. What's happening? Huh?"

He glared at Adrian.

"Bad juju."

"Knock it off, Rick," Adrian replied.

He stepped to the bay window and looked out over the village. His shop should be closed by now,

Margo in her nest on Jade Street, Summer doing God knows what.

"Want to walk to the shop?" he asked.

"Yeah."

Still in his travel khakis and new jogging shoes. Enrique chose a woolen knit from the coat rack by the door. Adrian, in slacks and Italian loafers, grabbed a sweatshirt and joined him to descend the rickety wooden stairs.

"We'd better move the stuff out of your safe," Enrique said firmly. "With the cops panting after you, you'd better be clean."

"Yeah. I guess so," Adrian agreed.

Once in the village, they veered away from the wharf entrance and strolled toward Ferrante's Jewelers.

Thirteen

DETECTIVE ISHIGURO LEFT KARIN in her room, talking on the phone to Summer. He'd assured her that it was okay to chat as long as she was back in time to meet with the police chief.

He returned to his room and walked onto the small balcony of the Venetian View, overlooking the beach.

The sun was setting; the shallow water near the shore had a lavender tint. He wished he'd packed his traveling watercolor set, or at least a camera. An art teacher once mentioned Capitola, about the light, how it was like the coast of northern Italy. Ah well, maybe I'll just sketch it in my pad and make some notes, he thought.

He settled into the lounge chair and watched people pack their things and leave the beach.

A long, low ribbon of fog began to roll into the bay.

SUMMER'S FINGERS TIGHTENED around the phone. She couldn't wait to tell Karin about her discovery.

"Well, after you left last night I kept thinking about those sapphires, so I got on the Internet, wow, I found this article. It's about how synthetic pink sapphires are being passed off as the real thing.

"So I printed it out," she said. "I'll bring it tonight. Mac's Patio is right next to the park on the Esplanade. Is Detective Ishiguro coming? No? Oh, okay. See you there."

Summer hung up and continued to gaze out the shop window, digesting what Karin had just told her. Karin's reaction confirmed her suspicions about those sapphires.

Boy, she thought, mom was shocked when she read that article…maybe now she'll see that slime-ball side of Adrian.

She picked up the article and read it again:

ALTERED SAPPHIRES FROM THAILAND VIOLATE STANDARDS, GEM EXPERTS SAY

CHANTHABURI, THAILAND—A sudden and inexplicable flood of sapphires called padparadschas has saturated the market in Chanthaburi, drawing gemstone dealers willing to pay more than ten times the going rates for the dazzling stones.

Industry officials are investigating the production of these famed rare orange-pink sapphires.

Padparadscha is the Sinhalese word for lotus blossom. The phenomenon has raised suspicion that certain Thai traders are doctoring lower-quality sapphires to mimic the real thing.

The suspicious padparadschas have uniform penetration of color, where most natural stones have uneven color zones, according to New York gem-store owner Ron Kager. Brilliant orange-pink hues are created by adding beryllium under extreme and intensive high heat.

Heating imperfect gems to enhance their color has been acceptable practice. But U.S. scientists charge that padparadschas are being altered with coloring agents, violating both ethical and economic standards.

Gem wholesalers stand to lose millions because of falsified gems.

Keeping up with the latest trick in the gem trade is at best "a constant game of cat and mouse," according to a spokesman from the American Gem Trade Association's Gemological Test Center in New York.

SUMMER'S BLUE EYES sparkled with excitement as she quickly walked to the office in the back of the shop to find Margo.

"Mom, Karin's back in town with a detective from LA. Mickey Brooks wanted her back to talk about that woman they found on the beach last night. I'm meeting Karin at Mac's Patio for a drink. You oughta come."

"What does Karin have to do with the death of that woman?" Margo asked. "Oh, that's right, when she left our house last night, she was walking toward the cliff path to her hotel … right? Do you think she had something to do with it?"

Margo heard the anxiety in her own voice. She sensed that things around her were changing too quickly and that made her uncomfortable.

"No, mom, she went straight home to Venice after she left us. She was attacked in her cottage. A detective from LA found her there bloody and half-conscious. And her cottage ransacked. And her camera stolen."

A soft breeze came off the bay, playing with Summer's long hair and Margo's wide-legged blue linen pants. Margo didn't mind the dress code Adrian had imposed on her. After all, Ferrante's was a high-end jewelry store with wealthy clientele from everywhere in the states and overseas. So the Eileen Fisher styles were what Margo wore. Conservatively muted mauves, blues, black and beige. Unstructured blouses and jackets, straight-legged pants or skirts. Nothing to compete with the sparkling gemstones.

Summer, the young fashionista, resented having to wear what she referred to as "classic old lady clothes" and would, on occasion, give Adrian fits when she showed up for work in decorated blue jeans and beaded cotton shirts.

Today, however, they wore the style that he wanted. Adrian's guests surely would come into the shop to see his latest creations.

They walked with confident enthusiasm, graceful and full of vitality, a striking difference from the tired, rumpled people leaving the beach after enjoying the warm, sunny day.

Summer reached into her tote bag for a scrunchie to control her hair and smiled at her mom. Hesitant, but curious, Summer asked, "Mom, I always wondered why both you and Adrian have those dragonfly tattoos on your hips. Anything to do with Adrian's sailboat— the Dragonfly? I saw Adrian's the other day. He was wearing a Speedo when he was out on the wharf."

"Oh, sweetie, people used to say that Adrian and I were joined at the hip, so one night when we were in The City on a buying trip we passed a tattoo parlor and, oh, God … we were having so much fun, so much good food and too much wine. We thought it was a great idea. We were laughing the whole time. We even had the tattoo artists, laughing with us. It's a wonder they did such a beautiful job."

Summer's expression darkened.

She had never questioned her mother about her personal stuff … but the questions were always there … now was a good a time to find out what she always wanted to know. "You guys? Were you lovers?"

Margo could feel herself getting very warm, her face flush. To her relief, one of their neighbors approached them. He was wearing an oversized fisherman's sweater and an old cap that he'd pulled down over his ears.

"Hi Weldon," Margo called.

"Hello Margo. Hi Summer. What a beautiful evening … weather for the locals, I always say. I'm sure you know all about the body they found on the beach. I hear she was a guest of Adrian Ferrante … probably drunk and fell of the cliff. Her family should sue him. He should have put a guardrail there. Well, now all those people he had as guests are staying at that new hotel by Soquel Creek … I hear Mickey is doing the investigating … A little excitement for Capitola … The media's all over the Jewel Box, TV and the papers. Well, have a good evening."

The elderly gentleman shuffled along to continue his evening walk.

"Bye Weldon, you too," Margo replied and turned to Summer.

"Is that what has you in a snit? This death on the beach? Are you worried about me? Don't be. Adrian and I, well things were different then ... Adrian and I were just into having fun, learning yoga, getting enlightened. When you'd go off to your dad's on holidays and for the summers, he and I spent a lot of time on his little sailboat, the first Dragonfly. Papa Ferrante and I both hoped that Adrian would ask me to marry him . . . but things changed when Papa Ferrante got sick. All the responsibility fell on Adrian to keep the store going and the cash flow constant. His focus began to change, from having fun to making money."

Margo and Summer were shocked when they saw Karin sitting by the window in Mac's Patio. Rather frail anyway, now she looked even more so, with her head partially bandaged, a bruise on her chin and a large dark purplish-blue spot showing under her huge sunglasses.

Concerned, they hurried in.

"Hey, you look like you need a drink," Summer exclaimed. Want some Prosecco while you read the article?" Summer handed the news clipping to Karin.

"No, not for me. Doctor's orders. Just some sparkling mineral water with lemon, thanks."

Karin leaned back against the booth and read the article.

"Well, this is fascinating. It could explain Mark's reaction when he saw you wearing that necklace, Summer. You still think this had something to do with Mark's murder? We'll need more than this article to prove anything. Do you suppose Adrian has something to do with altered sapphires?"

"I don't really know," Summer admitted. "But it could lead to finding an answer. Maybe."

She looked intently at Karin. "Are you scared?"

"No. If I wasn't so pissed off, I'd probably be frightened. I've been through some tough times before. Right now I just want to get to the bottom of this.

"Someone has it in for me," Karin said. "First, I'm set up to be guilty for Mark's murder. Then I get physically attacked and hit over the head. Then my digital camera's stolen. And now some woman winds up dead on your beach, and I'm being pulled into it."

Karin took some bills from her wallet, placed them on the table and scooted herself along the booth. "Anyway, I have to get back to the hotel by eight to meet with Detective Ishiguro and your police chief. I think Ishiguro, at least, believes in me."

Margo reflected on the conversation with Summer about Adrian.

"I know Adrian's capable of doing things that aren't on the up and up," she said. "Like this orphanage in Thailand … hmm, Thailand.

"You know," Margo continued, "before you meet with the detective, we could go to the shop and see if there are any sapphires I don't know about. But we'd better do it quickly. We'll go through the alley and in the back door so nobody will think we're opening the shop."

"Yeah," agreed Summer. "Let's do it. I know it's hard for you, mom, but maybe we can help Karin, and, who knows what we'll find out."

"I'm pretty nervous about this." Margo paused, then added, "But I agree, we should do it."

They paid the bill and hurried along Lawn Way to the back of the shop.

Margo's hands shook as she undid the burglar alarm and opened the door.

Summer gave her a reassuring hug.

"Mom, you stay out here in case someone comes."

Summer slipped into the partially lit shop with Karin close on her heels. Margo, worried and apprehensive, couldn't stand being outside alone and quietly drifted in behind them.

Karin hovered over the young woman as Summer deftly opened the safe, crouched, and moved books and papers aside. Glittering jewels caught her eye. Summer reached all the way in and discovered the small, jeweled gift box that Karin had given to Adrian before the party.

"That's strange. I wonder why he put this in here? Any chocolates inside? Nope, none."

Karin's curiosity was piqued when Summer opened the box. She asked if she could look at it. She began to pick at the sides, looking for a way to lift out the floor. She found a tab of fabric, and pulled. The bottom tilted up.

"Oh, my God," they exclaimed in unison. A hidden compartment was revealed.

There they were. Big and little orange-pink sapphires—hundreds of them.

Margo rushed over.

"I've never seen these," Margo said. "I don't remember them coming into the shop or even signing for them!"

The women heard voices at the front of the shop. Two men were coming inside. Karin recognized them immediately. Enrique and Adrian. She gasped. What were they doing here? I'd better get outta here, and fast.

She stuffed the jeweled box into her tote bag and raced to the back door.

"Gotta get back to the hotel to meet Dan and your police chief," she said as she left. "Maybe they can figure this out."

Margo slammed the safe shut and glared at Summer. Adrian confronted them, Enrique close behind. "Who was that, and what the hell are you two doing here after hours?"

"That young woman just took the jeweled box you had in the safe," Margo blurted. She was stunned by what she'd seen, and what she now knew. Instinctively, she tried to protect herself and her daughter.

Adrian's face flamed in rage. His fists were clenched. "What? Who is she?"

"You know her, you idiot!" shouted Enrique, roughly shoving Adrian and then Summer out of his way.

He ran out the back door after Karin and the Thank You Box.

"Margo, secure the shop. I'll deal with you later."

Adrian followed Enrique out the back door.

Now he remembered that skinny broad. She delivered the damned jeweled gift box to his house yesterday.

She was in the living room, he remembered, when I was on the phone. Did she overhear what I was saying? What does she know about this?

Summer, confused, hurting, turned in anger to her mother, "Why did you say that mom? Now she'll be accused of *stealing*, too!"

Margo locked the back door and waited until they'd walked out to the street before answering. "We hardly know that woman. I have to protect you and my job first. We'll have to tell Adrian that we were showing her some jewelry, and then she threatened us and had a gun or something."

A PARKING OFFICER interrupted them. "Hi Summer, Margo. You're pretty late closing, aren't you?"

"Oh, Ben, I'm glad you're here." Summer, close to tears, her arm sore where that man had pushed her, was really tired of all this. She beseeched him, "Please, call Mickey Brooks! A woman named Karin Blake is in danger. Adrian and another man are chasing her! Chief Brooks knows who Karin is. Could she get some patrol officers in the village to look for her?"

Adrian's soft Italian leather loafers kept slipping off. He was having a hard time keeping up with Enrique.

Enrique ran after Karin, pleased that he'd worn his new Adidas all-terrain running shoes. He spotted Karin turning the corner. That little bitch is running toward the beach, he grunted as he ran. Too bad Ratsami didn't finish her off.

Fourteen

KARIN THREW HER PURSE STRAP over her head and darted through the alley behind the jewelry store, racing past potted geraniums, surf boards and barbecues lining the deserted strip just off the beach. She knew the neighborhood well. Almost every summer of her childhood, her family had rented one of the bungalows that lined Lawn Way. She had played here often—safe, careless—washing sand from her feet before going inside. Now she barely caught a glimpse of its charm as she fled the shop, not sure which way to turn.

If Adrian and Enrique had decided to follow her, at this hour of the evening, she could be invisible in minutes. She ran toward the ocean hoping that in the twilight, she'd be able to get far enough down the beach. When she reached the beachside esplanade she looked back. Shock hit her. They were not far behind. They'd seen her and were closing in. Karin turned left and ran along the sand, immediately realizing she'd made a terrible mistake—she was headed in the wrong direction. She'd planned to go west toward the Wharf and the Venetian View Hotel to find Dan, her only hope. Now what?

Recalculating her options, she knew her only choice was to keep going and find cover. She headed in the direction of the surfers' jetty at the end of the beach. She knew she was taking a risk; if it was high tide, it might be a dead-end. In that case, the only way out would be to swim or scale the ten-foot wall into Esplanade Park above the beach. She put her head down and ran and ran, sand flying everywhere.

She reached the end of the beach and saw the tide crashing against the wall. Damn! There was no way out but up. Without a second thought, Karin dashed into the surf and began looking for a toehold. Her fingers found the jagged rocks that lined the wall. She remembered it, Capitola Fossil Rock. Indigenous to Capitola, the rock was scattered with shells and whalebones from the Miocene age. The cliffs were an archaeological treasure. But at this point, Karin didn't care if she destroyed the whole wall. She had to escape.

She began scaling, hand over hand. In seconds, she'd reached the midpoint. She knew what the two men wanted—the box. She reached in her bag and grabbed it. More afraid of them getting hold of the box than falling, Karin pulled it out and searched for a place in the wall where she could hide it. There were crevices everywhere that had been eroded over time. She tipped the box sideways and jammed it into a deep hole.

Wet and cold seeped through her jacket. Her injuries from the night before began to throb. Her tennis shoes were filled with water and made loud squeaks and groans.

She climbed the rest of the way up the wall, vaulted the railing and found herself in the park above the beach.

She ran down the stairs, doubled back onto the beach, now headed in the right direction.

She moved as fast as her legs would go considering her condition.

Breathing hard, Karin reached the wharf and pressed against a piling.

Her momentary sense of safety evaporated when she heard the thud of someone running, just yards away.

Enrique's angry face loomed over her. He gripped her arms and pushed her to the ground. He grabbed a knife from his pocket and pressed it to her neck. The blade was cold, menacingly sharp.

Karin's body went limp. With sand caked in her hair and mouth, she allowed herself to be pulled up without a fight. No use making this worse.

"LET'S GET OFF THE BEACH fast, I don't want to be seen by any locals." Adrian gestured toward the Dragonfly, bobbing by the landing under the Wharf.

"Not before we find out where she stashed the box. There wasn't anything in here," Enrique whispered, rifling through her purse.

"Let's not be so dramatic." Adrian cooed, looking into Karin's eyes. "She'll cooperate, I'm sure, won't you?"

"Just give us the box, Karin and this won't be so tough on you."

Enrique's tone shocked Karin. He was always such a pussycat at work, she thought—now he's scaring the hell out of me.

*   *   *

FROM THE BALCONY of his hotel room, Dan Ishiguro surveyed the horizon on Monterey Bay. The lights of a calamari boat glared on the water several hundred yards out. He noticed the group of buildings just below the hotel. Karin had mentioned them. The Venetian Court, Spanish-style stucco units with tile roofs, were the first condominiums in the state. Built in1924, each one sported its own individual flashy color, orange, lime green, lilac, lending a carnival atmosphere to the seashore.

He'd never been to Capitola, and couldn't believe a place with this air of small town innocence still existed. He could get used to this. Images of a life together with Karin began taking shape.

Whoa, partner, he thought, get a hold of yourself. I've never allowed these feelings associated with someone I'm investigating.

In his heart he really didn't believe Karin had killed Mark. She just wasn't the type. Besides, he hadn't been able to find even a shred of a motive in the last couple of weeks. She might be caught up in it some way, but he doubted it.

As his ruminations continued, Dan watched two men dragging a girl from under the wharf. She looked drunk, probably too much partying at one of the Esplanade bars. But, as he looked closer, his eyes adjusting to the early evening darkness, he could see it was Karin. One of them was her boss, Enrique Golden.

Years of training kicked in. Dan was out of his room, running toward the beach in seconds. He tried a gate by the Venetian Court. It was locked. He ran past it to the stairs that bordered the beach. They, too, were locked for the night. Looking through the gate, he could see the trio approaching the yacht moored at the wharf. Panic rose as he ran parallel to the beach, over the Stockton Bridge and down the Esplanade until he found an opening to the sand between two restaurants. By then, he was far down the beach. He slogged through the sand toward the wharf.

As he approached the pier pilings under the wharf, Dan saw a light flicker inside the yacht. Weighing his options, he decided to approach it from the water. He'd be less noticeable if he came up on the boat from below. Kicking off his shoes, he quickly ran into the surf. Get it over fast so you don't have time to think about it, he thought. He'd hated cold dark waters since his boyhood camp days, when the counselors taught water safety by making the boys go into a freezing, muddy lake and tread water for five minutes.

IT DIDN'T TAKE LONG for the cold Pacific waters to seep through his light shirt. He began to shiver.

Getting past the surf was easy; it was a calm night. He cleared the waves and began making his way to the boat. Within seconds, he had become ensnared in a kelp bed. Slimy strands of seaweed wrapped around his legs and arms and seemed to hold him in place. Dan panicked for a minute as he tried to clear himself. It was so dark in the water he couldn't tell which way to swim. The smell was nauseating, probably a combination of fish and decaying vegetation. He finally managed to paddle free with a long strand of seaweed clinging to his leg.

Just keep swimming you wuss, Dan admonished himself. He'd never had any patience for cowardice.

Approaching the boat, he took hold of the side and slowly hoisted himself up. He couldn't make it to the deck; there was no ladder. But he found a porthole. He managed to pull himself up and peered in. He could see Karin. She was disheveled and soaking wet. Her hair was matted with sand. Her hands were tied behind her.

He pulled himself up a little more, just in time to see Enrique Golden backhand Karin hard across the face.

Fifteen

AFTER HIS LONG WALK, Weldon ambled back up to his Jewel Box neighborhood. His arthritis was kicking in, no thanks to the incoming fog. As he came up the hill onto Aquamarine Drive, he spotted Adrian's neighbor Beverly unpacking the trunk of her car. He adored her. She was always patient and kind to him, treating him with great respect.

"Hello!" he shouted. He was happy to see her back from her trip to Paradise to visit her aunt. Paradise . . . he thought. Paradise! It was so hot there in the middle of the state, it should be called Hell.

"I bet you haven't heard about the excitement we're having up here."

Anxious to relate what he knew, Weldon offered to help Beverly carry her bags. Once in the house, he told her all about the party and the body found on the beach below and added that Mickey Brooks was interviewing all the guests "right now."

Beverly was always happy to see Weldon. He'd been so helpful after Harry died. He knew so much about the plants that grew in her garden. Gardening had been Harry's favorite hobby long before he had retired from PG&E. Weldon and Harry were good friends, and now Weldon kept things growing and healthy the way Harry would have. They put Beverly's bags in the front bedroom and walked out to the garden overlooking the beach below.

"Everything seems to be holding up pretty well after the heat wave you had here," Beverly smiled at him as she walked to the edge of the cliff. She looked at the scene below. Yellow tape still marked the spot where the woman died.

"Oh dear, how awful. Do you think the cliff gave way? Do you suppose she jumped?"

Beverly glanced back at Weldon, who was rubbing his chin.

"Say, Beverly, do you remember the security cameras we put up after Harry died? You think they might have caught something that could tell us what happened? After all you're right next door to Adrian's house."

"Good idea, Weldon. Adrian doesn't have security cameras out in back. He didn't like the way they looked on his fine old house. Wouldn't it be great if we helped Mickey solve this case?"

Weldon beamed, clearly blushing behind his grey beard.

They were equally excited. Beverly, a former City Council member for many years, still had a devotion to the city. Weldon, well, he just loved helping people.

The receiver was set up in a closet off the kitchen. Beverly opened the louvered doors while Weldon brought over two kitchen chairs. They sat down and looked at the instruction booklet together. The security camera had a wide angle lens with a motion detector that took in the distance up to 70 feet in varying light levels, 24 hours a day.

"Well, whatever happened, this should show it." Beverly put the tape in the TV and they began to view the video recording.

Sixteen

Eɴʀɪϙᴜᴇ ᴘᴜsʜᴇᴅ Kᴀʀɪɴ into one of the cabin chairs. Adrian grabbed a belt from the closet. They bound her hands to the back of the chair.

"She's awake," Enrique said. "Okay, where did you stash the Thank You Box?"

Karin, struggling to maintain her feistiness, spat out, "I don't know what you're talking about."

Adrian began to pace back and forth.

Enrique walked to the galley and picked up a dragonfly branding iron that Adrian used to mark his signature barbecued steaks. Flicking on the propane stove, he toyed with the iron, rolling it around in the flame. He smiled as the dragonfly insignia began to glow.

"Your time's up, girl. We know you took it. Margo said so and we know it's not in your bag. So, where is it?"

"Maybe she took it, whatever the hell you are talking about," Karin shot back, fighting back a growing fear.

"Look you little shit," Enrique said. "As if killing your boyfriend isn't enough, now you're a thief."

Adrian saw the tough approach was going nowhere. He slid next to Karin, put his hand on her shoulder and dredged up an avuncular tone. "Don't forget, our police chief is waiting to interview you about poor Roxy. Dead on the beach."

Adrian, pleased with himself, continued, "If you get me the box, I'll find you the best lawyer money can buy. I'm sure Rick will put down the branding iron, won't you Rick?"

"You're both crazy," Karin said. "I never killed anyone. I should have figured. I knew there was something odd about us having to deliver your lovely, little Thank You boxes, *Mister* Golden. You're involved in something really shady, aren't you? That's why you're using me as some sort of scapegoat."

She turned to Enrique. "Maybe you killed Mark. He was onto something. I saw photos he took of your gift boxes with phony bottoms. You creep, what did you do, break into my house while I was working at the caterers? I hope Mark gave you a good fight.

"And you," she turned to Adrian. "I know about those altered sapphires you've been handing off in your shop and about that rich-bitch fan club of yours. You two, chin deep in deception. Am I getting close? How long did you think you could get away with all this?"

She glared at Enrique. "You guys are going to get nailed."

"Shut the hell up. We'll see how tough you are. You fucking thief."

Enrique slapped Karin so hard, her head jerked to the side. An icy chill filled her chest. Her heart seemed to lodge in her throat and all she could do was gasp as tears filled her eyes.

Enrique's face reddened. "Listen to me you little bitch. Tell me where you put the goddamn box and we'll let you go. If you don't . . ."

By now, the branding iron was white hot. Leering at Karin, he leaned close and held it up. "Would this convince you?" He gave a low, sadistic laugh. As a boy he had great fun in Argentina finding stray cats and throwing them from the roof to see if they really did land on all fours. Enrique had relished the job of branding the cattle on his father's ranch. The squeal of the young calves in pain made him smile. And now, this little cow.

Karin's eyes widened. Fear sent chills to the nape of her neck and down her arms.

Enrique, no longer in control, reached out to grab her arm.

Karin strained away from the glowing iron and as she did her blouse slipped up, revealing the small of her back. Enrique saw the opportunity and, like a moth to a flame, pressed the iron into her flesh, leaving a two-inch, smoking dragonfly.

Karin's flesh sizzled. She shrieked, "Burn in hell, bastards," groaned, and fainted.

Adrian temper exploded. "Shit, look what you've done. That got us nowhere. You left my brand on her back. Damn you. Rick. I've had it with you!"

Seventeen

Ishiguro clutched the side of the Dragonfly, knuckles bleeding. Large chunks of seaweed hung from his waist and floated out behind him. The two men still hovered over Karin, shouting, but he couldn't hear what they were saying.

Karin looked scared. She was turned away from him but her body language told him she knew she was in trouble.

He released his grip and fell back into the water. He needed to get inside the boat. He wasn't going to wait for something worse to happen.

Choosing the stern as a safer entry, he began paddling around the back. He knew these huge yachts had sliding glass doors along the back so the guests would get a glimpse of the ocean without having to be outside.

The water felt menacing. Too many memories. He recalled his old technique for keeping panic at bay and kicked his right foot hard to keep himself high above the water. On the third kick, Dan felt something solid.

I'm not close enough to the pier, he thought. I wonder if that's an old piling?

He felt a large presence just to his right. He looked over and came eye to eye with a huge sea lion. The animal snorted, and sprayed a wet blanket of goo on Dan's face. He tried to take one arm out of the water to wipe his face, and immediately sank. He couldn't keep himself afloat with one hand in the water. The animal came at him with a fast jab. He grasped the lion's snout, an involuntary move he would regret.

He blinked his eyes open just in time to see the jaws spread and his arm disappear inside the creature's mouth. There didn't seem to be any pain, but Dan couldn't decide whether it was because of shock or a soft muzzle. Suddenly, he was being pulled down. Underwater, jostled, tumbled and beginning to lose his breath, he felt the animal turning erratically back and forth as if it wanted to pull his arm off.

Instinctively, Dan gave a hard kick and felt the creature move away.

He was still underwater. He had no idea where, how far down or even how to get up. He let himself go and floated slowly to the surface, gasping for air. The sea lion was nowhere in sight. He swam slowly toward the dock, trying to catch his breath and not cough. He'd taken in water, a lot of water. His lungs were nearly bursting.

Shivering, he hoisted himself onto the floating dock. He rolled over trying to get the salt water out and heaved.

The dock rolled rhythmically as Dan slowly recovered his breath.

A chill wind had set in. He began to shake. His eyes darted up; a face was staring at him from the wharf railing.

THE CALL CAME IN over her Nextel police phone just after eight. Mickey pushed the button on her lapel speaker. "Chief Brooks here."

"Chief, we've got word of a disturbance and possible foot chase in the Village. We're looking down from Depot Hill, been trying to locate the action. It looks like not much is going on, but a light's on in the

Dragonfly, a little unusual for this time of night. If you're in the wharf area, can you check it out?"

"Sure, I'm in front of the Venetian View, I'll proceed to the wharf and let you know what I see."

Although cars usually weren't allowed on the old wooden wharf, Mickey pulled the patrol car onto the planks and slowly made her way toward the Dragonfly.

Capitola Wharf, more than 150 years old, jutted into Monterey Bay far enough that it could be seen from almost anywhere in the village. It was the citizens' pride and joy. That night it was deserted, save one dozing fisherman with his fishing pole hanging over the railing close to the end of the wharf.

Mickey parked near the restaurant and began methodical inspections. She'd start with the wharf area and move to the Dragonfly. The Wharf House restaurant was closed and dark. Shining her flashlight in past the bar to the kitchen, all she saw were fishnets and buoys that decorated the place. After looking in the Bait and Tackle shop, she checked the wooden fishing boats that were hoisted out each night after the tourists left. Tarps covered some; she looked under those. On the other side of the wharf she saw that Sam, the boat rental guy, had caught several rock cod, which were swimming around in the old-fashioned fish tank for the kids to see.

She heard sounds from under the wharf so she walked to the side and looked over. It sounded like a harbor seal or a sea lion, such a nuisance, always lolling around creating trouble for the fishermen. She looked down and saw one on the floating dock, just behind the Dragonfly. Looking closer she realized it wasn't an animal, but a man. It took a minute for her to get down to him. He was breathing heavily, a gurgling sound coming from his chest.

"Lay still, sir, I'll get help. Try not to move until . . ."

Dan Ishiguro looked up. "Let me guess, you're Chief Brooks."

So much humor from a waterlogged guy, she thought.

"I'm Dan Ishiguro...Two men have Karin Blake inside that boat. I need to get in there. Help me up."

Mickey helped him to his knees. He paused, coughing and catching his breath.

"Damn," he whispered. "I'm trying not to cough but I swallowed a ton of that water."

"Detective, why don't you stay here and I'll go inside to see what's going on?"

"No way," he hissed, "We're going in there together. You're in first. I'll follow you. The best way in is the back sliding door. They're facing the other way in another area. Let's try to get in before they notice us."

The two crept onto the Dragonfly.

"Look, there's a gaff for spearing fish," said Mickey. "Get that, just in case we have a couple of big ones."

Dan removed his wet socks. He picked up the spear and carried it—like a Samurai, he thought. The vision of Karin being slapped flashed before him. His adrenalin surged. Why the hell is she in there?

Mickey gave Dan the sign. They opened the door and charged in.

Eighteen

LANGUIDLY, GEORGIA SHIFTED and moved one perfectly manicured hand over the natural wool blanket, hand-worked, from New Zealand. She appreciated fine things. Her childhood had been anything but deprived; *au contraire*, her doting parents had given her a golden life. Golden! With that, Georgia was fully awake, sitting upright on the bed, in the room she remembered so well. Adrian's guest room. Mama Ferrante always made Georgia so comfortable there, in the days when both women hoped that Georgia would become the new Mrs. Ferrante.

Georgia must have slept for more than an hour, she estimated, running her hands gingerly to smooth wrinkles out of her casual, silk running suit. Mustn't get a snag. Maybe she'd get a French manicure next time, no more talons. The burnt umber of her suit almost matched her painted nails and perfectly colored coif. Well, to be accurate, the umber was from her hairdresser's palette. She glanced toward the mirror to survey for damage, and spotted a photo on the shelf. Adrian, in sea-going whites, aboard the Queen Elizabeth I, leaning on the railing, martini in hand, Georgia at his side, then his parents and hers. How well she remembered . . . their engagement cruise.

But it was not to be. Georgia sighed. Now here she was back in Capitola after so many years, Adrian still a bachelor and she, ball-and-chained to Rick. Not to mention the horrendous mess about Mark, and now Adrian's aborted party. She mustn't allow any of this to tarnish her business reputation.

Where were the guys, anyway? No sound came from the rooms below. She checked—no one in the great room. She stopped at the bar to sample some macadamia nuts. Her stomach complained, hoping for something more substantial. She could ask the housekeeper, but no time for that.

Finding no trace of Adrian or Rick, Georgia chose a lightweight jacket from the hall tree and set out for the village, down the rickety steps, under the trestle and over the Stockton Street Bridge. The Dragonfly was moored at the wharf, she noted. The lights were on; the men must be having drinks. But she turned toward the village.

"Capitola's a sweet place," she mused, enjoying the vista from the bridge across the beach to waves crashing on the shore. "To think I might have wound up here instead of smoggy LA."

The wine shop was new, she noticed. And the horseshoe counter was gone from Polar Bear Ice Cream Shop. In a shop window, she read a t-shirt message: "Old Guys Rule." "Not if I have my way," she told no one in particular, and strolled ahead to the main drag, all two blocks of it.

She tried to remember shops from years back. No more pharmacy. No flower shop. No liquor store. She paused at The Craft Gallery, a trace of the Hippie Sixties with a bit of New Age tossed in, and . . . my, she thought . . . beautiful handmade pottery.

Her image flashed back from the window reflection. Where had the young Georgia gone, she pondered. All these years invested in Golden Catering. Was it worth the effort? Certainly her life with Rick was painless, but the bastard, all he wanted was her money.

If things had worked with Adrian, money would never have been an issue. No telling about sex. She'd heard from friends: Adrian still plays the field. But at least not like Rick . . . all he does is flirt and get laid . . . and not with me! An angry flush reddened her neck, old frustrations flaring.

Ferrante Jewelers. There it was, closed for the night. It looked about the same to her, stronger lighting enhanced the window displays, and posh but understated décor were Adrian's touch. "Papa" Ferrante, as children called Adrian's father, seldom left his jeweler's workbench. Creating pieces was his first love, after "Mama," of course.

Georgia gazed thoughtfully at the display. Clever of Adrian to tempt the evening strollers with high-gloss color photos. Gorgeous rings, she noted. Plenty of bling, only this was expensive bling. And that pendant, Adrian's fine work. It was set with yellow-pink stones that she couldn't identify. Not amber, for sure, or topaz. Where does he find such beautiful stones, she wondered.

Then, for the millionth time, she asked herself, what happened between us? Better yet, what didn't happen? Where did I go wrong? She'd wept over this loss so many times, and once again, her brusque exterior melted, her vision blurred. Oh Adrian, she cried to herself. Damn. Damn.

She passed the shop and went on to the Esplanade. Voices and music poured out from local watering holes, along with the wine and margaritas.

Georgia's thoughts turned to Mark Hansen. Just a few weeks ago, he'd been in this very village. I should have come with him, she told herself. Things might have been different. I could have seduced that handsome sucker up here, away from home. I could have shown Rick he's not the only trickster in the Golden family. Damn.

She stopped, leaned on the wall of a walk-up pizza joint, and closed her eyes, an unwelcome memory sweeping through. A dark memory, one that she wanted to banish forever. A memory that involved Mark. That last night with him in the little house by the canal in Venice. But no, the haunting returned. And now remorse swept in. If only I could turn back time. I didn't mean it . . . I didn't mean to . . .

A laughing couple came out from a bar and, seeing Georgia, stepped to one side. The girl chortled as they passed her:

"What's the matter, old girl?" she said. "Past your bedtime?"

Georgia stared vacantly. The insult didn't even hurt. It simply verified what she already knew: She didn't belong here. She must control her emotions, no more wallowing. "Grow up, girl," she chided herself. "You need to get honest with Number One—you." She had to get out of the village. Too many memories.

As she crossed the bridge, she heard the clink of wine glasses. The late dinner crowd dotted outdoor restaurant tables. A table knife clanked on a plate. From the wharf in the distance, the Dragonfly seemed to nod at Georgia.

Her flimsy gold flats started to rub uncomfortably. Well. I'm going native, she smiled to herself. She stepped out of her shoes and walked barefoot back out to the wharf.

The wind teasing her hair and caressing the silk trousers felt like a massage from Mother Nature. Spirits raised, she walked gingerly over wood slats of the wharf, eager to see Adrian, and even Rick.

At closer range, she could still see lights in the Dragonfly's cabin. Something exciting must be afloat, she decided. "Goody, I need a drink."

Nineteen

Swiftly, Mickey and Dan entered the galley. Enrique, surprised, immediately dropped the branding iron. Adrian regained his composure, stepped in front of Karin and smiled at Mickey.

"What are you doing here, Chief? My friends and I were just having a chat. Hey, who's this *gentleman*, and why is he carrying my fishing gaff?"

Karin's moans drew Dan quickly to her side. Seeing that her hands were tied, he began to remove the bindings. "Hang tight, Karin," he murmured, and as he untied her, Karin fully awakened. Although the burning pain in her back was overwhelming, she was relieved to see Dan. Her body shook. Her hands, now free, Karin struggled to lift her blouse and reveal the brand of the dragonfly, which now had turned to a deep red with black edges.

"Oooh," Karin gasped between sobs. "Look what they did to me!"

Sweat glistened on her pale face.

The sight of the ugly wound made Dan wince. He knelt beside Karin, looked into her eyes and put his arm around her shoulders.

Mickey Brooks aimed her gun at Enrique and Adrian. "Okay, you two, sit down at the table and put your hands on top where I can see them. So, Detective Ishiguro, this must be Karin Blake?"

Adrian didn't miss a beat. "He did that," he pointed at Enrique. "He's nuts! We just wanted to ask her some questions, and he got carried away."

"Wait a minute," Dan shouted. "We have a very injured woman here who might be in shock."

Quickly, he stuffed pillows under her legs, elevating them. He carefully covered her with a throw he found on the back of the couch, then checked her pulse.

"It's really racing," he announced. "She needs help, and fast."

With her gun still pointed at Enrique and Adrian, Mickey phoned her dispatcher and told him to get an ambulance over to the wharf immediately.

Just then they heard someone calling from the stern. "Woo hoo, Adrian, Rick. Are you in there?"

Georgia, tugging her blouse away from the wind, entered the cabin, calling out, "It's party time, and I need a drink." When she finally reached the open door of the galley she was startled at the scene before her. "Oh, no!"

THE SPACIOUS CABIN was filled with tension and testosterone. Georgia's eyes darted from Adrian past an unfamiliar man and woman, and then landed on Enrique.

"What's happening? I woke up and everyone was gone and I thought we'd have a drink on the Esplanade and now here you are with all these people—who are these people? What's happening?" she repeated, her words accelerating like a Vespa on take-off.

Mickey took a step toward Georgia and pointed to a club chair.

"Ma'am, sit down and shut up. And take a deep breath," she added, afraid the woman could veer into hysteria at any moment.

Georgia eyed the gun, then sat well forward in the chair, prepared to bolt if necessary. She glanced quickly around the cabin, noting the plush, carpeted floor, paneled walls, deep, comfortable couches and curtained windows. Recessed lights illuminated the tense scene. Her gaze fell on Karin Blake, stretched out on one of the sofas. Karin's face was tight with stress.

"Karin?" she gasped, "My God, why are you here?"

"Just hankering for a cruise, I guess," Karin managed. "Ask your husband, why don't you."

"Rick?" Georgia, her eyes wide, turned to her husband. "What are you up to? Dear God, if you've gotten us into trouble, so help me you'll regret it."

"Oh shut up, Georgia." Enrique glowered at his wife. "Karin's been nothing but trouble for us. Turns out she's a thief and that's not all. That little piece of shit murdered her boyfriend!"

"Not true," hissed Karin, through lips tight with pain. "Check out what your scumbag husband did to me."

Rolling to one side she pulled up her shirt.

Georgia recoiled at the sight of the red, raised outline of the dragonfly on Karin's slender back. Covering her eyes with her hands she moaned, "Rick, you're wrong. You're wrong. She didn't murder Mark. I can't stand it anymore. She didn't kill Mark. I did."

Twenty

TRYING TO COMPREHEND what she'd just revealed, Georgia stiffened and backed herself against the cabin wall. The guilt she'd repressed since that night in Venice was finally released and she began shaking, soft cries coming from her down-turned face.

"I feel like my life is falling apart. I'm glad I got this out in the open," she said in a hoarse voice. "That night—the night Mark died—I went to the house in Venice Beach. I knew Karin was working, and Mark would be alone. I had the idea that if I told him how I felt, he'd be glad. I didn't mean to kill him; I was actually in love with him. Of course, he didn't feel the same way. Mark had asked Karin to marry him. I couldn't understand how he could reject me. He would have had such a fabulous life with me to help him. I got so upset; it was the last rejection I was going to take. I picked up a bedside lamp and struck him in the head. He fell like a stone. He was all bloody. I got out of there as fast as I could. God forgive me!"

Her hands were clinging to the sides of her pants. She tore at the fabric, her eyes scanning the room, looking for signs of compassion.

"I guess I'm just a desperate old woman. I'm pathetic. I never thought I'd find myself in this situation," she whispered softly. "Karin doesn't deserve to be blamed for my lunacy; she didn't kill Mark."

Stunned silence filled the room.

"I could really use a drink, chief," Georgia said.

Karin spoke. "Mrs. Golden, this has nothing to do with Mark's death. Or at least I thought it didn't. Adrian and Enrique are involved in some kind of jewel scam and I've somehow gotten in the way. Don't tell me you didn't know about it?"

Georgia glared at Enrique, whose suave demeanor vaporized. Child-like, he averted his eyes.

"Tell me this isn't happening," she stated flatly. "What have you gotten into this time, you loser? If you're involved in something, Rick, we're done. This is the last time I'll bail you out. I won't be the only one going to jail."

Enrique sighed dramatically, "Georgia, Karin's just grabbing at whatever she can. She killed Mark. Adrian and I have the evidence, that's why we've been holding her." He glanced at Adrian for confirmation but received only a calm stare. "Adrian, I know you're trying to keep your pristine image, but now's the time to help me out here."

"You've backed yourself into a corner, Rick, my man. Don't try implicating me in something you have going on. I don't know what it is you've been up to, but you're not going to drag me into it."

Adrian turned to Mickey Brooks and said, "Mickey, you know I'm on the up and up. Just because this guy comes into town and begins flapping his mouth doesn't mean he knows what he's talking about."

"Hold on a minute, Adrian." Mickey had her hand up. "He hasn't really said much yet, let's hear what he has to say."

As Enrique opened his mouth, Karin turned painfully and said softly, "It's my turn, Mr. Golden. Let me see if I can piece this together. If you will let me, Chief Brooks, I think I've figured out what's been happening."

Chief Brooks discouraged her. "No, Karin, tonight's not the time. I want you to get to the hospital and have that burn looked at. I called for the paramedics. And besides, I want a tape of your testimony. I'll see you tomorrow at the station and we'll . . ."

Sirens interrupted her train of thought. She glanced in the direction of the wharf. In seconds, two female paramedics entered the cabin, looking around for their patient. "Who is it, Chief?"

"Over there on the sofa, Janet. She's been branded on her back. The burn looks pretty bad. I want her taken to Dominican and checked out. Call me as soon as you know anything, alright?"

"Branded? Jeez, you see something new every day," the paramedic responded. "This looks nasty, hey, what's with her head?"

"This isn't the first incident she's gotten into in the last couple of days. That's why I want her looked at. This woman was mugged, hit on the head and God knows what else. She's been through a hell of a lot and I wouldn't be surprised if she's in shock."

Dan moved toward the cabin door, "I'll go with her to the hospital, Chief, I think we should keep an eye on her. I'll have her at the station whatever time you say in the morning."

He glanced at Karin and thought, this case was getting complicated; sure came out of nowhere.

It took a few minutes for the paramedics to check Karin, move her onto the gurney and maneuver her out of the cabin to the waiting ambulance on the dock. As they drove away, two officers approached in a patrol car. Mickey returned her attention to Adrian, Enrique and Georgia, all standing around nervously.

"Sergeant, take these two men into custody, read them their rights—get 'em in separate cars. Hold 'em here in Capitola 'til I can get a handle on this thing. Ms. Golden, you're coming with me. I'll have to hold you, too. I don't want them speaking to one another or held in the same cell, understand?"

"Yes, Chief, do you want me to book them on anything?"

"No, just hold them for the time being on suspicion of kidnapping and assault with the intention to imprison and grievous bodily harm. That should be enough. They may contact counsel, if they choose."

"Chief, do you want me to use handcuffs?"

"Of course use handcuffs, I'm beginning to think we can't trust any of them."

Twenty-One

THINGS WERE QUIET At the Inn on Soquel Creek. Adrian's Army was getting restless. Sitting at a table under a Live Oak, Loretta tapped her fingernails on the tiled tabletop and rolled her eyes. " I swear, I feel like I'm in detention. Catholic school revisited! It's only nine-thirty, let's get out of here and find some fun, y'all."

Without hesitation, Elodia joined in and suggested a walk to the Esplanade. Sandi and Charlotte quickly agreed and the foursome gathered purses and wraps and headed for the village.

It was not a terribly long walk, but not suited for kitten heels and flip-flops. Nonetheless, the group soon found themselves standing outside of Zelda's, a bustling grill on the Esplanade. Live music poured from the open door. A peroxide-blond surfer-type danced up to Sandi and, grinning, spun her around before disappearing into the restaurant.

Sandi grinned, too. "Hey—I like this place!" She finished off the dance move with a bump and grind. "Let's go in!"

"Wait—up the street we can get margaritas," chimed in Elodia. "That's what I'm in the mood for."

She started off and the others, shrugging, followed. As they approached Margaritaville, Charlotte noticed a commotion ahead at the intersection.

Two police cruisers were stopped. Charlotte's eyes widened as she focused on the back seat of one car. Adrian! She nudged the others and all four gaped at the sight.

"What the heck is happening?" asked Sandi. "And who is that man in the other car?" In the dim light, it was hard to make out his features.

The cars moved on in the direction of the police station.

Loretta spoke up. "Maybe he's got to talk to the police some more about Roxy. You know what—let's go over to the wharf and see if we can get on the Dragonfly and wait for him to come back."

"I would love that," Sandi giggled. "I've never been on a yacht that big. It would be so fun!"

The others quickly agreed, and soon all four were picking their way down the worn boards of the Wharf to the mooring.

Tied in at the end of the wharf, the Dragonfly rocked gently on the dark waters. Lights showed faintly through curtained windows, but there was no sign of anyone on board.

"Hello! Permission to come aboard. Is anybody home?" Loretta called softly. Stepping back from the sliding main cabin doors she ventured, "I hope this is all right."

"Oh, c'mon Loretta. Let's go in." Sandi was really excited now, as she peered into the beautiful yacht.

They entered and, in unison, sucked in their breath. The modern décor was so very different from Adrian's antique-laden home on the cliff.

"Oh, my. Maybe we should take our shoes off." Elodia slipped out of her mules to luxuriate in the plush white carpet beneath her toes.

"Ooohh," Sandi ran her fingers along the large, curved crème ultrasuede couch. Mirrored walls of the cabin were framed with bleached teak paneling. Dimmed lighting in the ceiling and behind the couch and sideboard bar gave the room a soft, romantic feeling. The only sparks of color came from many jewel-toned silk throw pillows scattered on the couch. These were the colors of precious stones that Adrian incorporated into his unique creations: turquoise, emerald green, ruby red, brilliant orange.

Charlotte gracefully settled into a beige silk armchair next to a glass table displaying a most inviting bottle of Remy Martin XO Cognac conveniently accompanied by several Venetian glass snifters.

Sandi opened the refrigerator and let out a happy yelp.

"Dom Perignon!" she cried. "I know it's not a margarita, Elodia, but could you make do?"

Rummaging further into the fridge, she pulled out a tin of Osetra caviar. "Well, this just about makes it perfect."

A cupboard yielded champagne glasses. Soon the women were exploring the well-equipped galley, the passageways and cabins, all furnished for comfort and luxury.

Loretta bounced on the queen-size bed in one cabin, wondering if this was the one her husband shared with that tramp over the Fourth.

Who cared?

The champagne made her feel on top of the world, and besides, Jerry would pay, one way or another. He always did.

Back in the lounge, Charlotte popped the cork on another expensive bottle. Settling into the downy cushions, the women chatted about Adrian, his incredible jewelry that they all coveted, and the orphanage in Thailand.

Loretta looked sad. "I just love his jewelry. Each piece he's made for me makes me feel so special. But that's only part of it for me. Those orphans—I can relate. I haven't told too many people, but I was an orphan myself. Well, not really, but my dad split before I was born, and my mother couldn't deal, so I was raised in a home. I might as well have been an orphan. If Adrian was just yanking our chain about the Thai orphans, he's a real creep."

Suddenly the door to the lounge slid open. Startled, the women swiveled to see a uniformed Capitola officer filling the doorway. "I'm sorry, ladies. This is off limits. I must ask you to vacate the premises. And please take your things."

Elodia rose to her feet and tried a disarming smile. "We're friends of Mr. Ferrante," she began. "We saw him going off in a police car and thought we'd just wait for him here. He'd want us to make ourselves at home, trust me!"

The officer was not impressed. "As a matter of fact," he stated, "your friend Mr. Ferrante will be spending the night in jail." He held up a roll of yellow tape and admonished them, "Look, this is a crime scene and has to be secured. I'm afraid you have to leave."

The women, stunned, looked at each other. Finally, from Sandi, "Holy shit!"

They slowly gathered their belongings and headed for the gangway, Elodia clutching the half-empty bottle of Dom Perignon.

JOHN BURLEIGH STOOD by the reflection pond at the Inn and watched his wife running toward him.

"John!" she called out. "Buddy's run off again. One of the office staff told me she saw him trotting along Wharf Road, heading toward the village. Will you walk down there with me?"

"Okay honey, I could use a good walk. I told you that you gotta do something about that dog. Obedience training would be good for him … and maybe you, too. Oh, don't look at me like that. I could be really pissed off at you for getting involved in a mess when you know I have an election coming up next year."

"I'm sorry, John. I guess I got carried away. It was more than giving money to this charity. I was promised a gorgeous necklace as a gift from Adrian . . . I guess I'm not going to get it now."

"I know how much you like baubles, bangles and beads, honey, but ya gotta be more careful what you sign up for. Who turned you on to this non-profit orphanage thing anyway, and how much is it costing us?"

"Well, I pledged ten thousand. But don't worry; I haven't signed the check yet. Anyway, Loretta told me about it when I stayed at her villa in Montecito last month. I saw the piece she was wearing and just fell in love with the idea of helping an orphanage. I really am sorry.

"When I got to the party, I met Roxanne. I came across her in the bathroom, and she was crying, holding a glass of champagne. I asked her if she was all right. She snapped at me and got into a tirade about Adrian and his orphanage. She said that with all the money he's been getting from the members there should've been at least one already built. And all of a sudden there was Adrian, right there, soothing her with his charming smile, saying he thought she had too much to drink and needed a little fresh air. He turned to me and in a very firm but polite voice told me to please try the salmon that he had caught himself. Then he led her away—he really had a grip on her arm. Good Lord, do you think he killed her?"

"You know," John mused, "it might be a good idea to investigate this orphanage. I'm getting a feeling something about this stinks. Wait a minute. I can contact my guy in LA right now and get him to do some research. At least let's see if it has a non-profit 501(C)3 status. What's Adrian Ferrante calling this charity?"

Dana took the brochure from her evening bag and handed it to her husband. Opening his Blackberry, John made a call.

Feeling a lot better and really quite tender toward this big bear of a man, Dana put her hand around his free arm and the two headed along Wharf Road to find Buddy.

Outside the Shadowbrook restaurant, they heard the lively sounds of a jazz group and the excited buzz of people having fun. "Let's stop in there on our way back, after we find Buddy," an enthusiastic Dana said. "I've heard that Shadowbrook is the most romantic restaurant on the central coast. I'd love to check it out with you."

John finished his phone call, smiled at Dana, gave her a hug and agreed.

They continued to the village, with Dana calling out for Buddy. Passing the wharf, they noticed a flurry of excitement. Four women from Adrian's party were talking to a police officer. Dana looked at John, shook her head and said, "No, let's go find Buddy. I've had enough excitement with that bunch."

As they crossed Stockton Street Bridge, the sounds of the village's evening crowd grew louder. When they turned the corner, passing the front door of Margaritaville, they spotted Buddy. There he was, in front of Pizza My Heart, his tail wagging furiously as a young girl fed him.

"Buddy," Dana cried out. When Buddy heard her voice he came running. Uncharacteristically, John picked up the happily wiggling dog. Buddy proceeded to lick John's face with his greasy pepperoni-coated tongue.

John smiled at Dana. Still holding Buddy, he said, "You really gotta do something about this dog."

Twenty-Two

Karin rolled over on the bed and gasped as she sucked in a painful breath. Reality didn't take long to set in. She remembered the night before and felt along her ribcage for the large bandage the nurse had applied. She and Dan had been in the ER most of the night, witnessing various dramas being played out. One after another, gunshot victims, car accident survivors, domestic abuse, drug overdoses. It got sickening after a while. It turned out Karin's burn was only first-degree. The boys weren't as tough as they'd hoped. She was released with instructions to return in a day, when the wound would be dressed again.

She and Dan had dragged themselves back to the hotel around 3 a.m., and she'd been sound asleep ever since, thanks to Vicodin. She rolled onto her back and, hearing a small cough, jerked her head up. Dan was seated in the chair across the room, staring at her.

"I was beginning to wonder if you'd ever wake up. Your breathing worried me. Are you all right?" he asked, rising from the chair.

"I think so. I'm pretty groggy from those meds, but I guess it's not much worse than a bad kitchen burn."

"Well, I hate to roust you this early, but I promised the chief I'd have you at the station this morning and it's already ten. I brought you some coffee and breakfast rolls, a Pain D'Amande, a couple of Schnecken and a Bear Claw. They're from that awesome bakery, Gayle's, up the street. Think you could handle some food this morning?" He clearly hoped to get his hands on the stuff soon.

"Sure, I can handle it, but we have something to do before I eat. I'll get dressed if you step out for a minute."

Karin knew what she needed to do and hoped she had the strength to do it, and that it wasn't too late.

Outside the hotel, they walked slowly, Karin leading Dan over the bridge and around the Esplanade. Restaurants were getting their early morning deliveries of fresh produce, meat, wine and linens. It was an unusually sunny morning for the ocean-side area. People were out jogging, biking and walking their dogs. Dan noticed Karin's determined look, despite her obvious exhaustion. They cleared the Esplanade and went along the beach walkway. At the end, Karin turned onto the beach and began making her way across the sand.

"I put something here last night. I hope it's still there. If there was a high tide or a curious surfer, we're screwed," she mumbled, weaving her way past the early morning sunbathers and young Boogie boarders.

She made her way over the rocks at the end of the beach and looked up. Dan watched as she began to slowly scale the fossil wall. He was shocked at her energy.

"Karin, get down from there, I'll do whatever you need doing, just get down."

She ignored him.

Her hand found the box. It was wet and sandy and looked as if it had been hit by more than one wave.

She pried it loose from the hole and shoved it under her sweatshirt.

As she inched down the wall, Dan helped her onto the sand.

"So, what was so important up there, show me?"

"Not here, Dan," she whispered, looking around. "Let's move over to that area with the trees."

They found a spot behind the bandstand and sat on a concrete wall below the cliffs. She reached into her sweatshirt and pulled out a purple box decorated with jeweled flowers.

Dan had never seen anything like it. Where the hell did she get that?

His hand moved to touch the box, but Karin jerked back and held it close.

"I've been through a hell of a lot for this, Dan. I hope you understand if I'm a little jumpy about keeping hold of it. This may be the only evidence I have that could prove who killed Mark."

She looked around.

Seeing no one, she opened the box. "Move in a little bit more. I don't want anybody to see this."

The seawater had swollen the lid; it was hard to get off. She finally managed to pull it away and showed the contents to Dan.

He sucked in his breath.

"Wow!"

"Margo and Summer took me to Ferranti Jewelers last night, and we found this in the safe. I think I can prove there's been some kind of illegal activity between him and Enrique Golden, but I want to give my statement to the Capitola police. Do you mind if I wait to tell you? I'm still putting my thoughts together after what happened last night. I hope you understand. You've been so great to me and have been, well, like a friend through this whole thing. I want you to know how much I appreciate you sticking with me. I think you somehow believe in me. I hope this proves you right."

"No problem, I understand. Put that back in your sweatshirt and let's eat so we can get to the station."

Dan felt more relaxed than he had in days. He didn't really know why.

They walked to the seawall and sat on a bench, opening the white bakery bags and feasting on the buttery pastries and strong coffee.

Full and satisfied, they sat in the sun. Neither tried to speak. Dan realized Karin needed time to regroup before being interviewed.

The morning was peaceful and relaxing, just what they needed before the next intense scene at the police station.

OUT OF THE CORNER of his eye, Dan saw a flash of

black and white. He wheeled around, just a second too late. A sturdy Dalmation was loping away with the remains of their breakfast.

"Seamus, stop. Spit that out! Oh I'm so sorry. He loves used napkins, paper cups. Anything that's had food on it."

The woman standing beside the dog was tanned and healthy, the epitome of the California beach lifestyle. Her brunette hair was short-cropped, and she wore colorful pedal pushers over her swimsuit.

"Did he get any of your food? If he did I'll buy you something. It's no problem. I do it all the time. He's been known to grab whole slices of pizza out of little kids' hands."

She turned toward her dog. "Seamus, you're hopeless!"

"No, we were through. No harm done." Karin grinned.

Leaving the beach-dog mom to her reprimands, they walked toward the police station.

As they passed the old movie theater, sushi place and ice cream parlor, Dan began to realize he was really falling for this village. He could get used to the way of living here, everyone laid back and friendly, enjoying life.

They passed a jewelry store, and he thought about the box. No doubt it held the answer to a lot of questions.

Twenty-Three

KARIN AND DAN sat in the interview room at the station and waited for Chief Brooks to arrive.

"I'm nervous about this, Dan. It's my one chance to convince everyone there's something going on and that I'm innocent. Stick with me just a little longer, and keep your fingers crossed."

The chief entered the room.

"Hi Karin. Let's get down to business. This is just a preliminary interview. How are you feeling? Coffee?"

"I'm okay. Let's just get this over with."

"Go ahead."

"I'll start with the day I picked up some photos Mark had left for developing. They were taken shortly before his murder. They showed a young woman on a beach, wearing a low-cut dress. She had on an expensive necklace. When I got to Capitola to set up for the party, I went to the jewelry store to find Mr. Ferrante and saw the same girl from the photos. She turned out to be Summer Shepherd. We met later that night and she told me that Mark had taken photos of her modeling some of Mr. Ferrante's jewelry so she could use them for her portfolio."

Karin shifted in the chair and steadied the box under her sweatshirt. The burn was beginning to sting. She wished she'd brought along another Vicodin, but she continued, forcing herself to recall the details.

"Summer was scared. She said Mark had freaked out when he saw her wearing the necklace. He never told her why. Then when I met Margo, she told me she'd been curious about some of the jewels Adrian had been using. She'd never seen them come through the shop in the normal way, attached to invoices. Both of these women knew for months that something was strange. They protected this guy, some sort of twisted loyalty or something. No question, he's involved. My guess is he's been receiving jewels that were stolen or something."

"Describe the necklace," Brooks prompted.

"It was really big and gaudy, with huge pink rocks.

I remember thinking it was too grown up for Summer, looked too big on her."

"When you went in the shop did you see anything like it?"

"Yeah, several pieces seemed to have similar stones. None of them exactly like it, but close. After I set up for the Ferrante party and talked to the Shepherds, I decided I better get back to LA. I needed to check in with Dan."

She glanced at Ishiguro, looked back at Mickey Brooks and corrected herself, "Detective Ishiguro. And my catering work here was done. I got bored waiting for my plane and started looking at pictures in my digital camera. I was shocked. There were shots I hadn't taken and had never seen. Shots of the Thank You boxes from Golden Catering."

"What are those?" asked Chief Brooks.

"The Goldens are known for these ornate jeweled boxes full of expensive chocolates. They give them to clients just before a party. It's a prestige thing; everybody loves them. I delivered one to Mr. Ferrante before his party, as a matter of fact. I'll bet he has several, the parties he's given over the years. Anyway, the photos were strange because they'd been taken the day Mark died, August 17. I could see it on the window of the camera. He'd been waiting for me to get off work, and I thought when I first saw them that he just started shooting stuff to pass the time. But now I think he found something that he thought was strange. One of the shots showed one of the jeweled boxes open, and inside the bottom was tilted. It looked at first like someone was in the process of assembling it. But now I know it was a false bottom. I saw the box I brought to Mr. Ferrante in the safe at the jewelry shop. But wait, I'm getting ahead of myself."

Karin shifted again to take the pressure off her burn.

Mickey Brooks cautioned, "Karin, this can wait. We can finish the interview later."

"No, I want to get this out now. I've had enough of it all, and I want to prove I had nothing to do with Mark's murder."

She looked at Dan again and continued.

"When I got home from Capitola, I unlocked the door and went inside. Someone was waiting for me and clobbered me on the head. When I woke up, Dan was there. He took care of me, got me to the hospital. But the important thing is, my camera was missing. It was the only thing the guy took. I never put two and two together until I saw the same box last night. Summer had shown me an article about some fake Thai sapphires being smuggled into the United States. The photo in the article showed stones that look exactly like the ones in the necklace. They have a pinky-orange tone that's really distinct." Karin's face was flushed with anxiety.

She continued.

"Margo and Summer had the idea of going to the shop to see what we could find out. We found something all right—the gift box I'd seen in Mark's photos. That's when Adrian and Enrique came in. I ran out the back door. They followed me and I really got freaked, so I hid the box. They caught up with me and . . . well."

She hesitated, then went on.

"You know what happened to me on the Dragonfly. Those bastards branded me, Chief Brooks! They're barbaric! Please, please find out what's been happening and throw the book at them, they deserve anything they get!"

Karin reached into her sweatshirt and pulled out the box.

She placed it on the chief's desk. Mickey's eyes widened. She leaned forward.

Never taking her eyes off Chief Brook's face, Karin slowly opened the box, removed the bottom and revealed hundreds of vibrantly colored stones.

"This is what they branded me for."

Twenty-Four

CHIEF BROOKS STRAIGHTENED up in her chair, indicated for Karin to pause, and said, "This is major evidence. I need to keep this. Let's take a break. Stay nearby, Karin. Detective Ishiguro, obviously this is pertinent to your investigation too. I'll put the box secure in our safe."

Karin and Dan stepped outside. Chief Brooks motioned for an officer and closed the door.

"This is getting juicy," Chief Brooks said. "We need to get Margo Shepherd over here pronto, and her daughter Summer, too. Phone them, tell 'em you'll pick them up in ten minutes. And tell them to bring along that article about sapphires from Thailand. Thanks."

She opened a bottled water and leaned back in her chair, eyes closed as she reviewed events of the past few days. Adrian and all those women. All those parties. The suspicious death of a guest . . . was she pushed over the cliff? If so, by whom? And Karin Blake. Seems straight-ahead. Ishiguro seems to trust her.

Was there more to her connection with the Goldens, other than hired help . . . and what was her boyfriend up to, really?

Adrian Ferrante, now there's a strange duck, Brooks mused.

Mr. Beautiful or Mr. Ugly, who was he? And this Enrique Golden, not your typical caterer. And where does Georgia Golden's crazy confession fit in? Clearly, she's the money behind the business. Some marital strife between the two. Maybe Karin's story is legit. We'll see. Maybe Margo can help clarify this mess.

She remembered that Congressman Burleigh's wife was at Adrian's party. Burleigh and his aide had arrived yesterday. Is he involved, too, for criminy sakes?

THE CHIEF'S REVERIE EVAPORATED as an officer escorted Margo and Summer into the room.

"Please have a seat," said Chief Brooks.

The women nodded.

With the jewelry shop temporarily closed, they had spent the evening and morning trying to piece their stories together and listlessly watching a classic Humphrey Bogart movie. Summer had sympathized when her mom expressed anger at Adrian, and at Karin.

How could they have left her clueless, Margo had complained.

Testify? What was she supposed to talk about?

Finally, the police chief called on them.

"Karin described what she saw in the safe at the jewelry store," she said, "and mentioned an article that you, Summer, showed her about sapphires from Thailand. Did you bring a copy of that article? What do you know about the sapphires at Ferrante's"

Margo remained seated, looking straight at Chief Brooks, but on her lap, her hands moved nervously. She described her long employment with the Ferrantes, and how wonderful the family had been to her. She had no idea anything was out of the ordinary, she said, but was surprised at the sight of so many unusual stones, gems not in the inventory.

"What kind of stones?" asked Chief Brooks.

"Yellow, golden, pinkish. Lots of them. Now I've learned they may be sapphires."

She answered the chief's next questions. "I do all the accounting and pay the bills for Ferrante's, but no, I haven't seen invoices for the stones in question."

The chief then turned to Summer, who smoothed imaginary wrinkles from her Hawaiian print sundress and fluffed her hair. Slowly, she opened an envelope, removed the clipping she'd copied from the Internet, and handed it to the police chief.

"Yeah," she began, "I knew that Mr. Ferrante had some rad stones in his store. That was why I said we should go to the shop last night. I was, like, shocked when Karin found that Thank You Box thing from the catering company in the safe. That's when I went, hey, smuggled rocks, maybe."

Chief Brooks unfolded the article, studied it, and put it aside.

Summer continued. Her boss did make great jewelry, especially the individual pieces for the women supporting his Thai orphanage project. "His *supposed* orphanage project," she added wryly, holding back her opinion of the "airhead" women who flocked after Adrian.

* * *

A LATE MORNING easterly breeze ruffled John Burleigh's thick brown hair as he stomped across the parking area in front of the Capitola Police department, his aide James Evans hurrying along behind.

"Looks like we've got ourselves a nice morning, Congressman," said Evans. He gazed longingly toward the bay. "It would be nice to stretch out on warm sand and soak up some rays this afternoon."

"Forget it, Jim. We've got to get Dana quietly extricated from this mess. I've got meetings in Washington next week."

Burleigh ran large well-manicured fingers tiredly through his hair. His bulk filled the doorway as they entered the station. Evans followed up the rear, carrying a leather brief case.

"Congressman John Burleigh here." He presented his card to the clerk seated at a desk behind a glass partition. Burleigh's presence brought the clerk to attention.

"Yes sir?" She glanced at the card. "What can we do for you?"

"It's important I speak with Police Chief Brooks." Although he didn't say "immediately", the implied tone got the clerk on her feet.

"I'll see if she's available now, sir."

The clerk disappeared down a hall behind her desk. A few minutes later she reappeared and led Burleigh and Evans to the chief's office.

"Make yourselves comfortable, gentlemen," said Chief Brooks. "Congressman Burleigh? I'm Mickey Brooks. What can I do for you?"

"Let me have that fax, Jim."

"It's a pleasure to meet you, Congressman Burleigh . . . and . . . ?"

"My aide, Mr. James Evans."

Mickey Brooks nodded. She turned to Burleigh. She thought he looked very tired but impressive. "Your wife has been very helpful, very forthright, I may need to see her again."

Burleigh interjected "Yes, yes. Of course. Unfortunate business . . . I flew up to be with Dana as soon as I heard. I wasn't exactly aware of this group Dana was joining. She often lends her name to various charities, but she knew I was particularly busy with affairs in Washington just now. So we hadn't had the opportunity to discuss this organization.

"Anyway, my office ran an extensive check this last twelve hours based on information from Dana's brochure. This fax here indicates, so far, no legal arrangements have been made with the Thai government, plus our Embassy in Thailand has no record of any dealings with an Adrian Ferrante. But customs records show he traveled to Thailand several times to purchase gemstones. The amounts involved were not unusual for a successful small town jeweler."

Burleigh snorted.

"Frankly, that Ferrante has a whole bevy of brash broads flush with more money than sense fluttering around him. He manages to charm and mesmerize every one of them.

"Can you imagine?" Burliegh went on. "Even Dana was halfway in his thrall.

"This Thai orphanage sounds like smoke and mirrors to me. Once I understood how much money the ladies were expected to fork over each year for membership and there was no business plan, well, I began to suspect the orphans were some lonely women and the orphanage might be a good-sized yacht named the Dragonfly. By the way, I've requested an FBI report on Mr. Ferrante and his activities. They'll send you a copy for your files, too."

"Well!" commented the chief. "You're certainly making my job easier. I really appreciate your help, sir. Though I'd still like your wife available."

"We're glad to help in any way," said Burleigh. "The sooner this is all cleared up the better. Dana hadn't actually given Ferrante any money, you understand. She agrees it would be foolish to be mixed up in this, unless it's on the up and up. She has a deep interest in orphans around the world.

"Of course, I'd appreciate it if her name could be kept out of proceedings as much as possible. You understand. This could be particularly embarrassing for us. You do understand?"

"Of course." Mickey Brooks extended her hand, thinking, you bet I understand.

The congressman stood, and held out his business card. "By the way, my aide Jim here will be on top of things. You can reach him in my LA office if you need any help. I have to be in Washington in a couple of days, but Dana will be around if you need her."

"I certainly appreciate your help, Congressman Burleigh. Thank you."

Mickey Brooks rose, handed him her card, and walked Burleigh and Evans to the front of the station.

She bade them good-bye, smiled and quickly retreated to her office to read the fax and review the latest developments.

"What a long morning," the chief exclaimed as an officer came in. "The Goldens' attorney will be here from LA any time now and Ferrante's attorney has been waiting in the lobby for two hours, We need to start wrapping things up."

She paused, and added, "I'm starving and I need a break."

Giving the officer a "you take charge" look, she stood, stretched, and continued, "In the meantime, I'm going over to Papa O's for lunch."

Twenty-Five

"Okay, Karin, we've been excused by the police chief. She might want us back later, though." Concerned, Dan added, "Want to go back to your room and rest?"

"No, thanks. You've been just great. But I need some fresh air. Want to walk up to Depot Hill? There's a great view of Capitola, the beach, the wharf, the trestle. You can see over to the Jewel Box neighborhood, and Pleasure Point."

"Sounds good to me. What's Pleasure Point?" he asked.

"That's where they surf big time."

"I used to surf," Dan offered shyly. "But haven't had time lately. It'd be fun to try it again."

Karin nodded, thinking he'd be a great surfing partner.

Their walk ended mid-village, when Dan's cell phone rang. Good thing, thought Karin, glancing at the concrete stairway leading up the hill. She'd counted the steps as a kid. Eighty-five. I'd never make it up those babies today, the way I feel.

Dan steered her to a nearby bench. "Let's sit here and I'll get this call."

"Hello? Yes, Sarge. Good news? Wow, how about that. Yeah, she's sitting right here. Yeah, Nick, you're right about that. She will be happy to hear it. Yeah, you're right about that too."

Dan winked at Karin and smiled. "She is kinda cute and very resilient too. Pretty strong for her size. C'mon, cut it out. This is no vacation. One more thing to clear up and we should be back in LA tomorrow. Okay, thanks for the heads-up."

Karin shifted her weight on the hard bench. The burn was becoming uncomfortable again. She looked quizzically at Dan.

"I'll be happy to hear about what?"

"Well," Dan took her hand. "It looks like they picked up a Thai national who matches the description of your assailant. Apparently he was speeding down

Pico Boulevard and ran a red. The cops who pulled him over noticed the tattoo on his neck. Anyway they did a routine check, opened the trunk and found your camera and a big bag of pink stones.

"After a strenuous interrogation, he caved and implicated Enrique Golden as his contact. They also found several knives in a gym bag, and sent them to the lab for testing."

Tears of relief filled her eyes. "That's so amazing. Is it possible there's a connection between the Thai guy and Mark's death? And maybe what's going on up here? Oh, Dan, thanks for believing in me."

"Look, I'd love to go for that walk, but I need to get back to Mickey Brooks. Why don't you go back to the hotel and get some rest. We'll take that walk later. I'd really like to do that."

Karin squeezed his hand and got up slowly. "You know, you're right. A little more rest. This has been an exhausting couple of days."

She smiled and almost giggled with delight. "This is so amazing."

Dan felt a sense of relief as he made his way to the police station. The call had given them the break they'd been looking for. Now he had to figure out how this guy in LA fit into this mess.

Chief Brooks was in her office. "Come in. We have a lot to talk about. Congressman Burleigh paid me an interesting visit this morning. Do you know anything about this Thai orphanage that Adrian supposedly founded?"

"Yeah, Karin explained it to me, I guess she heard about it from Margo and Summer. Seems he gets rich women to contribute to it by inducting them into some sort of club or something. Then gives them a fancy piece of jewelry to tie the knot."

"Well, there's no Thai orphanage. And there's no non-profit either. Seems Adrian has cooked up some scheme to bilk these women out of tons of bucks. The only problem is, from a prosecution standpoint, he gave them those jewels in exchange for the money. I'm not sure we can make a charge stick. We might be able to get him on fraud for saying he had a non-profit. I'll have to ask the DA."

Dan agreed. "The guy's something else. A real piece of work."

He eyed the M&M's in a jar on Mickey's desk, wondering if he could open the lid and take just one.

"I got a call from my desk sergeant in LA. They picked up a guy on a routine traffic stop. He matches the description of the man who assaulted Karin the night she got back from Capitola. They searched his car and he had a Sony Sure Shot camera. It's the same one taken from her that night. The I.D. matched. And, here's the topper. They found a three-pound bag of sapphires in the lining of the trunk. This guy is a hit man for the Thai mafia down there. The sapphires are a big part of their operation. They're fakes."

"Well, doesn't surprise me." Mickey fiddled with the pen on her desk. "I just got the article from Margo and Summer. It talks about this very thing. We need to figure out which of the Goldens is handling them for this guy.

"I wonder if Adrian knows he's in possession of fake gems? Probably thinks he's getting a great deal on the real thing. I almost feel sorry for the guy. What a dolt. He's no chip off the Ferrante block, that's for sure. His father and grandfather supposedly were great guys."

Dan reached for the M&M jar. "The Goldens were staying with Ferrante last night before everything blew up. Can you get me a search warrant for his place? Also, one for the store. Let's see what else we can find. I have a strong suspicion this whole deal has something to do with Mark Hansen's death. Wonder if it'll tie into the death here in Capitola?"

"I'll phone the courthouse. I need an order from a judge. Here, read this article while I make the call."

Twenty-Six

"I<small>T'S</small> A <small>PRETTY WILD COLOR</small>, huh?" Dan, in the passenger side of Mickey's Ford Escort, looked up at Adrian Ferrante's Victorian house. It was painted a bright coral.

"Well," said Mickey, "it's been that color forever. The family's owned it since it was built in 1895 and the color has never changed. It really stands out from the beach."

They approached the gate; Mickey rang the bell. "Yes, may I help you?" came the female voice. "Chief Mickey Brooks of the Capitola Police. We have a search warrant for the premises. Open the gate, please. We'll be waiting for you at the front door." The buzzer sounded immediately and they quickly made their way to the ornately carved oak door. It opened and they entered the foyer. "Mr. Ferrante isn't here, I don't know if I should allow you in," protested an older woman, obviously the housekeeper.

"There's no allowing. We have a warrant here, and we're going to search the house." Mickey was calmly forceful. She presented the warrant. "Best if you go to the kitchen area and stay there. We'll let you know when we've finished. And please, don't touch anything."

The woman backed up, turned and scurried off. "Mr. Ferrante isn't going to like this."

Mickey glanced up the stairs. "Since Enrique and Georgia Golden were guests here, their stuff might still be in a bedroom up there."

Dan led the way, two steps at a time

Mickey kept up and said, "I also want to check Adrian's study, see if there's anything about this orphanage business."

They found the guest bedroom. The suitcases, still full, were open on the bed. Each began searching, one taking the suitcases, the other, the rest of the room. It was as if they'd worked together for years.

After checking the suitcases, Dan moved to the briefcase propped near the desk. Within seconds, he produced a laptop and turned it on, not sure where to start. Scanning the opening screen he saw several icons. He thought, if I knew what I was looking for this would be a lot easier. He started at the top and clicked on "Photos."

There they were, one after another. The photos Karin had described, taken by Mark at Golden Catering. The jeweled box ajar, the bottom askew.

"I have something here, Mickey." Dan was excited now. Finally, it was all coming together. "Look! The shots Karin told us about. Oh we're gonna nail these guys."

"Yeah." Mickey looked thoughtful. "It's going to be tough on Adrian. He's well-liked in this town."

She opened the closet door, flicked on the light and reached for a jogger's jacket on a hook. She pulled something from the pocket and held it up. Take a look at this . . . Enrique's cell phone.

Dan took the phone and checked the number log. Adrian's number was there, not surprising. But the kicker was identity of a cell phone caller. He took out his wallet and retrieved a piece of paper. He'd jotted down the perp's name, Ratsami Naris, when he'd talked to the sergeant from his department. Bingo, the same name.

"Pretty slick, huh? This is as clean as it gets."

Mickey gave a thumbs up. "Let's go down to the study."

It didn't take long to find the file with information on a Swiss account. Mickey and Dan were certain it would disclose deposits coinciding with the date of each of the women's jewelry acquisitions.

They told the housekeeper they were leaving and headed for the village.

DAN PARKED THE CAR in front of Ferrante Jewelers and looked around out of habit. "Did you get the key?"

"Yes," Mickey answered. "Margo Shepherd gave it to me this morning. I hope we find something. I'm convinced Adrian is involved in this, and I need substantial proof. It'll make it easier for the DA."

They entered the shop from the back. Keeping a low profile was part of Mickey Brooks' approach. After all, this was a small town, no need having more mouths flapping than necessary.

"Did Margo give you the combination to the safe?" Dan asked.

"Yeah, she didn't want to but I convinced her with the search warrant."

Mickey made quick work of the lock and opened the heavy door. Inside were several boxes and trays.

The two began methodically going through them.

"Look at this necklace!" Mickey held the sapphire piece to her neck. "Wow, not Adrian's normal inventory. It's huge! Who would wear something like this?

It's probably for one of his philanthropic posse-girls."

She passed it to him. "Judging from the size of those stones and the amount of gold this baby must retail for over 50K. This is in a league by itself. More Rodeo Drive than Capitola-by-the-Sea."

Dan held the necklace carefully. "Keep that out, it might be useful. Let's see what else we can find."

Mickey reached to the bottom of the safe and pulled out a purple felt bag.

"It's heavy enough. Maybe this is what we're looking for." She opened the drawstrings and dumped the contents onto a felt lined tray. Dozens of the fiery fake sapphires spilled out like marbles.

"Thank God, I thought we were going to come up dry. At least they can get him for fraud. And who knows, there may be more charges for the bogus orphanage. Let's get back to the station. We need to work this out and call the DA."

Twenty-Seven

"WELDON, WAIT! I KNOW YOU'RE EXCITED about showing this to the chief, but slow down." Beverly's sensible Easy Strides made the walk to the village and under the trestle easier, but Weldon kept several paces ahead. "I just hope the chief's not angry with us for holding onto this overnight. I couldn't sleep knowing that we didn't turn it in right away."

"Look, Bev, it was pretty late when we finished. Plus, the police were busy down on the wharf. I'm sure it'll be okay. After all …"

They reached the station. Weldon paused, spotted the police chief getting out of her car. Impulsively, he called, "Mickey we've got a tape. You gotta look at it right away. It's about that body on the beach!"

Mickey looked surprised. Beverly looked worried. Mickey could see that both Beverly and Weldon were out of breath. Whatever these two had might be important.

"Okay, let's take a look."

"Be with you in a minute," she addressed Dan, standing nearby. Then to Weldon and Beverly, "There's a VCR inside." She took the tape. What's this about?"

Beverly sighed, "It's from my security camera. It was Weldon's idea to see if it picked up what happened next door the night of the party."

Weldon beamed with pride as Mickey slipped the tape into the VCR. The three of them stood back to watch.

In the lobby, Dan shifted his weight from one foot to the other. What information could those two possibly have for Mickey Brooks, he wondered. And who are they?

Dan turned and went outside.

Traffic was light under the trestle to the beach; summer was over, he realized as he sat on the uncomfortable, but handy, bench near the lawn outside the police station.

He looked up at the wooden trestle spanning what he guessed must be Depot Hill and the Jewel Box neighborhoods, with Soquel Creek flowing beneath. Wow, he thought, that trestle must date back a while.

The back door of the museum opened, a tall woman stepped out, locked the door and walked toward him across the parking lot.

Willowy, he thought approvingly. He called to her. "Excuse me, would you know anything about the railroad trestle?"

"Yeah, a thing or two," she answered. "It could also be considered a trussed bridge, and wooden trusses go back to the Greeks and are mentioned by Italian architects in the Sixteenth Century.

"But trestles like this," she continued, "go back to the 19th century, mostly in mountainous areas to cross rivers. See the structure under the rail? In bridges that don't have the space underneath, the support has to go above . . . pretty cool, huh?"

Dan figured she could go on and on, but she hurried into the City Hall.

Fine with me, he thought. I need some time to think.

Good thing those two locals came along to occupy Chief Brooks for a while. He was glad Karin included him in her search for that candy box. Even with damage from the night air and sea spray, the box was impressive. The caterers must have some high-class clientele.

Dan pondered, how many jewels had Enrique Golden smuggled in his fake-bottom Thank You Boxes? Speaking of Golden, good work on the LAPD's part, finding that Thai guy. Good help from Burleigh, too. Whew, he thought. Complicated business. Sounds like the LA part of this is clear, but what about Capitola. Just how far was the jeweler Ferrante implicated, especially in his guest's death fall off the cliff. Some house, Ferrante's.

Dan's thoughts retraced his search with Chief Brooks.

Could there be more to this mess?

Dan noticed a woman with dark, spiky hair walking under the trestle. It was Karin in fresh jeans and a crisp white t-shirt, full of smiles for him.

"Whoa, what a surprise." Dan leaned back. "I didn't expect you. Mickey's busy with some local folks and I needed some air. Want to join me?"

Karin looked much better, he thought, hoping she'd had a nap.

She smiled. "I just had the best . . ."

Agitated shouting from inside the police station cut her short.

"You idiot!" came a man's voice from inside the station. "Now look . . ."

"Don't say a word!' came a shrill cry.

Karin's eyes widened. "Here we go. Sounds like the party's started."

Back in the station lobby, Dan and Karin encountered two disheveled men, a distraught woman and three deadpan "suits".

"Must be their attorneys," muttered Dan. Karin nodded.

"There she is, the murderer." Enrique pointed at Karin. An arm in a pressed suit reached out to restrain him.

"Don't respond," Dan whispered her way.

A scornful glance from Enrique warned Georgia to keep her mouth shut. Without makeup, Georgia had put on at least ten years. She began pawing in her purse. Triumphantly, she pulled out a brush and began on her messed hair.

It hadn't been a good night. A village jail cell with no room service wasn't Georgia's idea of acceptable overnight accommodations. She glanced at her husband, his suit rumpled, hair askew. His world had turned dark. Poor baby. Ha. She had no sympathy. Under her breath, Georgia muttered, "What a jerk, pulling poor Adrian down with him. I never should have introduced those two."

Adrian, still reasonably tidy after a night on a hard cot, leaned against the wall, not speaking, his ordinarily bronzed face pale.

Enrique lunged again, the restraining hand reached out again, but he shook his attorney loose, approached Adrian and shouted, "Can't you do anything right? Fucking with those bitches, scattering jewels like birdseed?"

One obscenity after another tumbled out. The office door opened and the police chief entered the lobby with two elderly people.

The tension was palpable. Mickey glared at Enrique. "Enough," she growled. He was tamed, somewhat, stepping back. The others turned to the chief.

"I have something here I want you all to watch," she said. "Come with me." She turned back to the office. Georgia took one chair; Ishiguro steered Karin to the other. The men packed themselves in, as Mickey started the video.

The images were surprisingly clear. For a few minutes all they saw was a clutch of finches vying for seeds from a bird feeder at the cliff's edge. From the house, Adrian appeared, escorting a beautiful blonde to the pergola. She wobbled, trying to keep up with him in her strappy stilettos.

The police-station viewers turned as Adrian's voice broke through. "Wait a minute here. Where'd you get this? From my nosy next-door neighbor over there?" He pointed at Beverly, who flinched, then bravely countered, "Just watch, Mr. Ferrante."

The video camera tracked the couple as he steered her toward the edge of the cliff, guided her to a bench, and began to rub her shoulders.

Enrique sneered at the jeweler. Georgia glanced at Adrian, groped in her purse and extracted a handkerchief to dab at her nose.

Adrian, in the video, had turned back toward his house and was walking away, leaving the woman alone. She braced her feet and lifted herself from the bench. Then she walked, more like wobbled, to the edge of the cliff. She tottered for a moment, turned abruptly and looked back at the house. Almost gracefully, she began to sway, glanced back toward waters of Monterey Bay, and appeared to lose her balance.

The viewers gasped.

The woman, Roxanne Webber Reynolds, arms flailing at the air, began to fall backward, like an unprepared skydiver, to the beach below.

A sigh of relief from Adrian.

A snort from Enrique. "You got off on that one, fella."

Another gasp from Georgia.

The attorneys stood, impassively.

Chief Brooks broke the silence, thanked Weldon and Beverly and sent them on their way.

"Well," she breathed. "This evidence frees you in one matter, Mr. Ferrante. I am certain this will clear you and all your guests of any suspicion in the untimely death of Roxanne Reynolds. But I must alert you that incriminating information involving both you and Mr. Golden has come to us from the LAPD and other sources."

Briefly, she described the arrest of the Thai man, evidence on him, his police and prison records, and some details about the smuggled sapphires. She reached in her pocket, and pulled out a cell phone for all to see.

"This is yours, Mr. Golden," she said quietly. "It contains information connecting you with Ratsami Naris, who confessed to the murder of Mark Hansen, and implicated you."

"Where'd you get that?" Enrique blathered. "That's not mine, someone must have planted it."

Mickey replied calmly, "Search warrant. Adrian's house. Your jacket pocket."

She turned to Adrian.

"We also have sufficient information linking you and Mr. Golden to the smuggling of adulterated sapphires from Thailand. You will remain in custody, pending arraignment."

One attorney stepped forward. "On what charges are they being held?"

"Aggravated assault and battery for starters," Mickey answered, "and then possibly fraud, smuggling . . . care to add anything else?"

Without replying, the "suits" left the room.

Adrian and Enrique were escorted out by police officers.

Mickey smiled at Georgia. "You are free to go, Mrs. Golden. Next time, I'd advise you not to attempt confessing to something you didn't do. By the way, why did you think *you* killed him, when you *knew* he died of stab wounds? You said you hit him over the head with a lamp."

"He was stabbed?" Georgia stared at her husband.

Enrique raised his hands, palms up, "It was in the Times the next day, you nitwit."

Georgia slumped. "I just couldn't read it. I thought I knew what happened."

Georgia's attorney put a consoling hand on her arm. "As Chief Brooks said, you're free to go."

Georgia thought fast. She'd have to check in at the Inn for the night, she guessed, and get back to LA tomorrow on her own. But, she told herself, she could handle all that, and a lot more.

Mickey turned to Ishiguro. "Thank God this is out of my hands now—yours, too. We've done some good work here. I'm sure we'll talk during the week to wrap this thing up, and we'll probably meet again in court."

Finally, Mickey touched Karin on the shoulder. "A terrible ordeal for you, Ms. Blake, too much abuse, both here and, I understand, in your hometown. I hope you come back soon. You deserve a chance to enjoy sunnier days in Capitola."

Flashes from the past several days interrupted Karin's thoughts as the police chief spoke. Mostly she recalled herself trying, just trying so hard. Trying to do her job for Enrique and Georgia, trying to figure things out with Margo and Summer, trying so hard to remember what happened on the Dragonfly. Longing for Mark.

She glanced at Dan.

Mickey smiled and began to leave the office when, on second thought, she turned back. "And Karin," Mickey added sympathetically, "Again, I'm so sorry you had such a bad experience in Capitola."

Twenty-Eight

KARIN TOOK ONE LAST LOOK at Capitola Village before she and Dan left for the airport. She reminded herself that she promised to return—next time to relax.

It was a good day. Traffic was light on Highway 17, their flight was early and good seats easy to come by.

Karin sat by the window, ready to get home. Jennie had promised to start cleaning the Venice bungalow. Things would be okay pretty soon. She pulled out her cell and dialed LA.

Jennie had left a message: "Hi there. Your place is all ready. Call me when you get in, we can grab a burrito for dinner."

Karin smiled at hearing the message.

Ah, Jennie.

"My twin and my best friend," she explained to Dan, then thought, but you've been my best man friend since Mark.

He smiled back. After the rush of leaving Capitola, this was their first chance to recap all that happened. "How're you holding up?"

"Fine."

"Your back?"

"The salve is working, no pain."

A flight attendant leaned over to wish them an easy trip, her thick black hair held back in a French braid, attractive against Southwest's easy-wear uniform. Almost immediately, the plane began to taxi.

THE BOEING 737 CIRCLED San Jose and flew south over the coastal mountains. The land seemed to wait for winter's rains.

"So what're you thinking about," Dan asked, his gaze directed to the front of the plane.

Karin glanced at him. "Oh, just trying to sort it all out. How it all unraveled. What's next. And how that son of a bitch found the barbecue brander in the first place."

"How did you know about the holes in the seawall?"

She shifted uneasily in the reclined seat.

"When we were teenagers, the area under the cliff was called the Pump House, only the local kids called it the Stink House. I guess it was an early sewage system or something. There was a space between the Stink House and the cliff, where the locals, who called themselves the 'Tola Rats, used to hide, smoking pot. If the tide was out, they'd go down on the sand and try to climb up to the Stink House. It was kind of a clubhouse for them, so of course we visiting kids wanted to be part of it all. As kind of an initiation, we climbed that front wall, with rocks full of fossil shells. Pretty cool."

"And were you accepted?"

"Yeah, but we were there only two weeks. I always hated to go back to LA."

"And that candy box. Amazing."

"Yeah, who would suspect the false bottom. Mark took a huge risk photographing that. Ever since I saw them, I wondered why he took those pictures. I thought he was just bored originally. But now I know he knew something was up, and it was the reason he got killed. Enrique must have been watching him on the security cameras.

Dan thought for a moment.

"Those guys will do time, for sure. Especially Enrique—setting up Mark's murder, smuggling, kidnapping you, and then physical assault and battery."

"And after all that, Georgia came out clean," Karin mused. "I never trusted her. Calling me anorexic, ha."

"You are a bit of a wafer," Dan teased. "Need to fatten you up."

WITH A BUMP, the attendant stopped the cart at their row. Karin opted for diet soda, Dan for orange juice. Famished, both demolished their peanuts. "This oughta do it," she muttered.

"What was your first impression of Ferrante's orphanage scheme?" Dan talked as he munched.

"I forgot to tell Chief Brooks what I heard Adrian saying on the phone when I was at his house," Karin said. "It sounded threatening. Guess I figured it was some business deal. Deal, indeed. What a scam. And all those rich biddies handing over their husbands' cash."

"But Congressman Burleigh came through," Dan continued. "He didn't seem that bad a guy."

"Well, he's still not getting my vote," Karin emphasized. "Too much 'good ole boys' baggage for me. Guess I'll have to write him a thank-you, though. He really did come through great."

As their plane neared LAX the two traced, detail by detail, the implications of the catering company's jeweled Thank You box, the Thailand jewel scam, and the tarnishing of the Ferrante name.

"What about the women in the jewelry shop?" Dan asked.

"Margo and Summer? I realized I was too judgmental about them protecting Adrian, so I phoned Summer. I'm going back to spend some time with them after I get my life straightened out."

INSIDE THE AIRPORT, Dan reached for her overnight bag. "You're riding home with me, right?"

Karin shook her head. She searched his face for approval. "No, my sister's coming to get me. She phoned this morning. My parents have been worried sick."

Parents? Dan hadn't heard mention of parents. But of course, how long had they known one another? A week?

He reached in his satchel.

"In that case, I have a little something for you. Sweets for the sweet, and all that."

He handed her a box.

She looked down at a fancy box, "Chocolates!"

She leaned over, and kissed his cheek.

"I'll phone you tomorrow."

Epilogue

SIX MONTHS WENT BY in a flash. In Capitola Village, early spring meant fewer tourists, except on sunny weekends when visitors still crowded the small shops. Weekdays, locals reclaimed their territory and enjoyed the peace and quiet.

Weldon and Beverly took to meeting at five for a brisk walk through the village before she cooked a homey dinner for him. Everyone noticed that Weldon was adding a few pounds, and that he wore a frequent and contented smile.

At the police station, Mickey Brooks sat at her desk and reflected on the events of the previous August. Now, Enrique was incarcerated in LA, and Adrian was cooling his heels in the County Jail, awaiting his trial for smuggling, fraud and kidnapping. They'd both do time for sure. Mickey allowed a faint smile.

"We did all right for a small town," she thought. "Shame that Adrian screwed up. Lucky thing Margo Shepherd stepped in to manage the jewelry store, even though Adrian's designs are gone."

Mickey was aware that Margo frequently visited Adrian at the jail, and no one could miss her new wheels, a tasteful white Mercedes coupe with tan leather upholstery.

Margo herself was enjoying the challenge of keeping the business going, but she dearly missed her daughter.

Summer had taken a deep breath and left for LA to try to break into modeling, or even an acting career. She kept up her new friendship with Karin Blake; the two met often for lunch at a taqueria.

Karin spent a few weeks recovering, eating, sleeping and pulling herself together. As her old self resurfaced, she began looking for a new direction. She landed an entry-level job writing for the food section of the LA Times.

Dan found this amusing, as a high percentage of the meals Karin cooked for him were pretty much inedible. He put up with them, nevertheless; she had other good attributes.

Once in a while, Karin ran into Georgia Golden, who was running the catering business by herself while she waited for her divorce from Enrique to become final. Georgia made donations to John Burleigh's re-election campaign, and displayed a campaign poster in her office that showed the congressman with his arm around his smiling wife. Burleigh also was smiling, and holding a small terrier.

Adrian's flock of philanthropic women had scattered, but sporadically kept in touch. Elodia received a postcard from Charlotte, vacationing in San Tropez. In a flowing script Charlotte had written "Darling, I've found the most amazing jeweler!!!"

Margo's Eggplant Parmesan Casserole

THIS DISH CAN BE USED as a side dish or main course and is great for a hearty luncheon. You can add anything you have in the refrigerator—turkey, chicken—or put it over pasta.

1 large eggplant, peeled, cut crosswise
    into ¼ inch disc shapes.
Salt
1 medium onion, diced
1 stalk celery, diced
1 red or green pepper, diced
4 or more cloves garlic, finely minced
8 large white mushrooms, sliced
2-3 tsps. dried basil
2-3 tsps. dried oregano
3-4 Tbsps. olive oil
2 cups marinara sauce
8 oz. container skim milk ricotta cheese
1 egg, lightly beaten
2 tsps. parsley, finely chopped
½ lb. thinly sliced skim milk mozzarella
1 cup Parmesan cheese, grated
½ cup provolone or Romano cheese, grated

Lay the eggplant slices on a baking tray lined with two layers of paper towels. Salt generously, turn and salt the other side. Let sit for at least ½ hour or more. Wipe off excess moisture and salt with more paper towels. Press down firmly to extract moisture.

Preheat the oven to 350 degrees. Use a 9- by 13-inch baking dish.

Sauté the onion, celery, pepper, garlic, mushrooms, basil and oregano in the olive oil until soft but not brown. Add the marinara sauce and simmer for 15 minutes.

Mix the ricotta with the beaten egg and parsley. Begin layering the casserole by spooning 3 large tablespoons of the sauce mixture in the bottom of the baking dish. Make sure there are lots of mushrooms on the bottom.

Place the eggplant slices next, overlapping until the bottom of the dish is covered.

Spoon all of the ricotta mixture over the eggplant, covering it as much as possible.

Sprinkle half the Parmesan over the ricotta mixture.

Layer the mozzarella on top, then the provolone or Romano over that.

Cover with the remaining marinara sauce and then the remaining Parmesan.

Cover tightly with aluminum foil and bake for one hour.

Author Biographies

Marybeth Varcados: A retired newspaper journalist, she still loves writing and editing. She and her husband have been Capitola residents since 1968. Their two daughters grew up with the beach as their playground.

Judith Feinman: Born in Brooklyn, New York, and has lived in Capitola California since 1985. She was a member of the Capitola Arts Commission and the Board of the Santa Cruz Art League. Judith, a watercolorist, is an active member of the Santa Cruz Watercolor Society and the Coastal Art Alliance. Her husband of fifty years, married children, five grandchildren, painting, photography, gardening, writing and being a member of the Women of Mystery fill her days with great joy.

Pat Pease: Reformed New Englander, retired RN, determined and plucky gardener who forgets each year that you really can't grow a good tomato in cool and salty sea breezes. Lives just over the border from Capitola in Santa Cruz with patient husband Hugh and their peculiar cat, Jasper. Mother of three bright and loving daughters, who brought home fine sons-in-law; grandmother to four fun grandchildren.

Tomi Newman: Retired high school English teacher and curriculum developer, retired volunteer ESL tutor trainer, involved mom of two, grandmother of five and wife of one and only, born and raised in San Pedro by the sea, but retired to the redwood beauty of Santa Cruz County twenty-five years ago.

Gayle Ortiz: Content Capitola resident for 27 years. She is a bakery owner, community activist and clothing designer. She lives alongside Soquel Creek in a 1930's home, Riverlodge, with her husband, two cats and a dog.